MW01717034

THRONE OF THE PHOENIX

KINGDOM OF FAIRYTALES ALADDIN BOOK 3

J A ARMITAGE

R CASTRO

Copyright © 2020 by J A Armitage

All rights reserved.

No part of this book may be reproduced in any form or by any electronic or mechanical means, including information storage and retrieval systems, without written permission from the author, except for the use of brief quotations in a book review.

Please contact the publisher Info@enchantedquillpress.com for translation and audio rights

www.enchantedquillpress.com

Edited By Rose Lipscomb

Cover by Enchanted Quill Press

Proof Reader: Tina Merritt

❀ Created with Vellum

KINGDOM OF FAIRYTALES

You all know the fairytales, the stories that always have the happy ending. But what happens after all those storybook characters get what they wanted? Is it really a happily ever after?

In this prequel, you will find out what happens next, be transported back to those lands you fell in love with and be prepared to meet some new characters along the way.

Kingdom of Fairytales is a new way of reading with one chapter a day and one book a week throughout the year beginning January 1st

Lighting-fast reads you won't be able to put down

Read in real time as each chapter follows a day in the life of a character throughout the entire year, with each bite-sized episode representing a week in the life of our hero.

Each character's story wrapped up at the end of every season with a brand new character and story featured in each season.

Fantasy has never been so epic!

READING ORDER

Kingdom of Fairytales is a 52 book series split into thirteen seasons. Each season has a four book story arc of a fairytale character with the last season seeing them all coming together. You can read any series first with the exception of thirteen, however it is recommended that you read in the order below...

PREQUEL

SLEEPING BEAUTY

1. Queen of Dragons
2. Heiress of Embers
3. Throne of Fury
4. Goddess of Flames

LITTLE MERMAID

5. Queen of Mermaids
6. Heiress of the Sea

7. Throne of Change
8. Goddess of Water

RED RIDING HOOD

9. King of Wolves
10. Heir of the Curse
11. Throne of Night
12. God of Shifters

RAPUNZEL

13. King of Devotion
14. Heir of Thorns
15. Throne of Enchantment
16. God of Loyalty

RUMPELSTILTSKIN

17. Queen of Unicorns
18. Heiress of Gold
19. Throne of Sacrifice
20. Goddess of Loss

BEAUTY AND THE BEAST

21. King of Beasts
22. Heir of Beauty
23. Throne of Betrayal

ALADDIN

25. Queen of the Sun
26. Heiress of Shadows
27. Throne of the Phoenix
28. Goddess of Fire

CINDERELLA

29. Queen of Song
30. Heiress of Melody
31. Throne of Symphony
32. Goddess of Harmony

ALICE IN WONDERLAND

33. Queen of Clockwork
34. Heiress of Delusion
35. Throne of Cards
36. Goddess of Hearts

WIZARD OF OZ

37. King of Traitors
38. Heir of Fugitives
39. Throne of Emeralds
40. God of Storms

SNOW WHITE

41. Queen of Reflections
42. Heiress of Mirrors
43. Throne of Wands
44. Goddess of Magic

PETER PAN

45. Queen of Skies
46. Heiress of Stars
47. Throne of Feathers
48. Goddess of Air

URBIS

KINGDOM
OF
FAIRYTALES
URBIS PRISON
BADALAH
DRACONIS
DESERT
ZHORE
KISBU
SHIPLEY
THE VALE
AZREN
MOSA
ABORIA
ELDER
URBIS
AZURE
ENCHANTIA
AIRE
SKYLA
EMERALD CITY
OZ
FLORIS
TULIS
THE FORGE
ARCADIA
RENAIS
MELFALL
ATLANTICE
ANTLA
W
E
S

1ST JULY

The kingdom of Badalah shone like a crown in the desert, and Kisbu was the jewel in the center. The sun glinted off the domes of the palace as we came in to land. The giant airship of the Urbis Express lowered slowly in the sky, finally resting with a slight bump on the ground at the station.

All around the station, people were running, fear etched onto their faces.

"What's happening?" I said to the conductor who merely shrugged. I craned to see what everyone was running away from through the small windows. All I could see were people, all running toward the center of Kisbu. Hesitantly, I stepped down from the airship, and almost immediately, I was swept out into the crowd.

"Go home," I whispered to Asher. "I'll see you there." Asher rose into the sky as I was jostled along, caught up in the tide of fear. It was only as the gates of the palace came into view that it became apparent that these people weren't running from something but to something. They were crowding the palace, banging on the gates, shouting at the guards who stood at the other side of the gates. I pushed through to the front.

"What's happening here?" I shouted through to a guard, but he didn't even acknowledge who I was, let alone respond. Whatever was going on, I wasn't going to get answers here. Nor was I going to be let into the building. Fortunately for me, I'd been sneaking out of the palace at night for a year. It meant I'd also been sneaking into the palace. Pushing through the swathes of people, I heard them chanting for food. They were hungry, starving even. Young children were among them, the elderly. All the people my parents had sworn to protect were now crammed together in anger. The back of the palace wasn't as crowded as the front, but there were enough people there that would see if I climbed the vines I normally used to get over the walls. All it would take was one person to see me, and then they'd all follow. The palace would be swarmed with people. Angry people who were currently muttering threats about my mother.

As I continued on around the perimeter, I remembered another way into the grounds. A way my father had taught me not too long ago. He'd crawled through a gap in the wall, invisible to everyone as it was hidden behind a bush. I picked up my speed, keeping my hood up so no one would recognize me. Not that I knew if they would if I walked through them wearing full ceremonial costume and shouting my name, but I wasn't going to chance it.

When I was sure no one was looking, I dove into the bush and through the gap. Before anyone had the chance to see me, I followed the path my father had shown me down to the underbelly of the palace. From there, it was only a matter of walking into the main cellars and up to the palace. It was eerily quiet, a stark difference to the bedlam outside the walls. Fear gripped me as I wondered if anyone would remember me. My mother flitted in and out of her memory so often, and that was before I'd left for days.

As I walked through the palace, the sound of my shoes echoing off the marble floor was a poignant reminder of my situation. I was alone. The noise of the crowds outside remained, though, a distant chanting getting louder, the closer I walked to the front of the palace. I headed to the one man I needed to see more than anyone. Maybe he wouldn't remember me, but I remembered him. I was halfway down the corridor that housed his suite when someone called my name.

"Jamal!" I said when I saw who it was. I ran to him and almost fell into his arms. Almost, but not quite.

"What's happening?"

He pulled me away from the window that looked out over the front of the palace.

"I don't want them to see you," he said by way of explanation. "They aren't very happy with the monarchy at the moment."

"I can see that. Why? What's happened? Are they still mad that my mother held a party in the name of the out of towners?"

"I wish it was that simple," Jamal replied. He pointed to a set of stairs to the second floor. "Come on, I should show you the extent of the problem before I tell you what the problem is."

The stairwell was dark, and it was only as we began to climb the stairs that I realized why. The curtains covering the windows that opened out onto the royal balcony were closed.

At the top, Jamal pulled them back an inch to give me a view of the people outside. It was much worse than I feared. The balcony had been built for the royals to stand on and wave to the people during special occasions. From it, the view stretched on down Kisbu's busiest street for miles. It had been designed that way to allow as many people as possible to see us. It also meant that from here we could see them...all of them. People by the thousands filled the streets in every direction.

"Everyone in Kisbu is out there!" I exclaimed, stepping back from the curtain.

"Not quite," Jamal added, "but most of them. They are hungry. There's no food."

I ran my hand over the back of my neck, rubbing it to comfort myself. "We fed them a few days ago. Kisbu has plenty of food. They can't all be hungry."

"We fed the poor a few days ago."

"These aren't the poor?" I asked, confused. If they weren't poor, why were they protesting for food?

"You said it yourself. Most of Kisbu is out there—rich, poor, and everyone in between."

"I don't understand."

Jamal took my hands in his. "When you left, there was food in the shops. Now the shops are closing. They cannot buy food from the farmers. People who can afford food cannot get access to it. The whole of Kisbu has shut down. The gates are closed. The people of

Kisbu closed them to stop the out of towners, but now they can't get food in."

"You mean the people did this to themselves? Why doesn't Mother just demand that the gates to the city be opened again?"

Jamal slowly shook his head. "It was your mother that ordered them shut in the first place."

Now I was really confused. "Why would she do that?"

"She's gone, Gaia. Or at least, the memory of who she is has. Completely. Since you left, I've seen none of the woman I once admired. She was sad that you'd gone, but when I asked her about it, she couldn't articulate the cause of her sadness. When I said your name, there was no flicker of recognition."

This was my fault. Talking to my mother wouldn't help. If what Jamal said was true, the only way to bring her back was to solve this whole problem. The problem of the magical curse that was blighting our kingdom. I just wish I knew how to fix it. I sneaked another peek through the gap in the curtains. So many unhappy people. How had we spiraled into this in a matter of weeks? Then I saw something that tore my heart in two. Right near the gates, at the front of the crowd, was a man dressed in rags, not the Sultan's uniform I was used to seeing him in.

"My father is out there!" I said, turning to Jamal.

"Aladdin?"

He joined me at the window, and I pointed out the pathetic looking figure at the front. My father was practically eye-to-eye with one of the guards. The men he had personally hand-picked to serve the royals.

"Do we have food?" I asked.

"You don't need to worry on that score, Gaia. The kitchens are well stocked."

I turned and began to run downstairs.

"Where are you going?"

I paused, turning my head back to face him. "I'm going to open the gates. I'm going to let them all in."

"Are you serious?" Jamal said, chasing me down the stairs. But I was too quick for him. I knew what I was about to do was insanity. We'd be swamped, overrun with people, but I'd made a pledge to serve my kingdom. I might not be the Sultana, but I was the only royal in the palace who hadn't lost their mind.

In the main entrance, a lone figure stood at the doors. Peering through the glass.

"Freya!"

She turned around. Her face lit up immediately when she saw who it was. She ran toward me, but stopped short about five feet from where I stood. Her face lost its excitement, and her expression turned to one of worry. Her eyes darted to the side, just over my left shoulder. When I turned around to see what had gotten her attention, I saw Jamal just behind me shaking his head. When he saw me looking, he stopped.

"What?" I asked.

"You can't open the gates, Gaia. Look at the people out there. They are out for blood."

"They are out for food, and I'm going to give it to them." I turned back to Freya. "Can you go down to the kitchens and tell them to bring everything we have into the main hall?"

"Everything?" she asked quietly, looking more at Jamal than me.

"Everything!" I reiterated. "Jamal, find a guard. Take them to my mother. I'm assuming she is in her room. I want to make sure she is safe if things do turn nasty."

Jamal walked around me to stand between me and the door. Just behind him, Freya watched on with tears in her eyes.

"Turn? Open your eyes, Gaia. Things are already nasty. If you'd have stayed here to deal with this mess rather than go off gallivanting to Urbis, you'd know how bad it's got."

"I can see for myself how bad it is, but my father is out there."

"Your father doesn't even know who you are!" Jamal shouted.

I stood stock-still, not used to the way he was speaking to me.

"I know who he is," I replied, standing my ground. "Now, please do what I ask you. I'm still in charge here."

He put his hands on his hips, blocking my way.

"Move...now!" I looked into his eyes, which had taken on a hard edge. He was taller than me, so I had to incline my head slightly, but I wasn't going to back down.

When it became apparent he wasn't going to move, I casually walked around him and opened the door to the palace. No one was going hungry while I was in charge, no matter what Jamal said.

The crowd jeered as I walked down the stairs to the gates. The noise rumbled through my ears, making me wonder if I was making the right decision, after all. But then I saw my father. While all those around him were shouting, he was still. He looked at me with such sadness that my heart broke.

"Open the gates!" I said to the nearest guard. At first, I thought he'd forgotten who I was, but then, I realized the look of incredulity he was giving me had more to do with my request than who I was.

Inside the guards' hut, was a horn. It was used to announce ceremonial affairs to the public. Today was far from a ceremony, but if I could get at least some of the people's attention, then it would have to do. I ducked in, found the horn, and ran back up the stairs to the palace doors. Inside the open door, the entrance hall was empty, which meant either Freya and Jamal had acquiesced to my requests, or they had gone and hidden somewhere. I held the horn to my lips and blew with as much force as I could muster.

Immediately, the crowd quietened.

"People of Kisbu," I shouted. "I know you are hungry. I know you are scared, and I know you are angry. I'm going to open the gates of the palace to feed as many of you as we can. I hope to open the gates to the city too and solve the problems we are having. Until then, I invite you all to come and have a meal on us. I only ask that you line up in an orderly manner and take only what you need. We also have a limited supply of food, and I'd like as many of you to eat as possible. I want you to be assured that I'll be doing everything I can to solve the situation so that none of you go hungry in the future. Guards. Open the gates."

My heart almost stopped as the guards did what was asked of them. Despite my assurances, I wasn't sure how the crowds would react. I was in the doorway of the palace. If they wanted to overrun the palace, I'd be trampled in seconds. But as I watched, the people did exactly as I had asked, shuffling themselves into an orderly line once they were within the palace grounds.

I watched my father take his place at about twenty people back. I gave him a smile that he didn't return. When the man at the front of the line got to me, I ushered him inside.

"This way, ladies and gentlemen. I've asked the kitchen staff to bring food into the great hall. There are two doors, one at the front and one at the back. I ask that you take your food and move through quickly to the back exit so that others can get food too."

Freya was in the hall with some of the palace staff. Long tables had already been set up, and the kitchen staff was busily bringing food in. It was a long cry from the banquets we usually put on in the grand hall. There were no decorations, no tablecloths or place settings. There were not even chairs for people to sit on, but there was food, and that was all that mattered.

I extended my hand in invitation for the people to go in.

"Freya!" I shouted as the people began to file past me. She turned her head in my direction and placed the platter she was carrying on one of the tables. I beckoned her over.

"Can you go to the other side of the hall and escort the people out once they've got enough food. They can walk the far corridor and out of the staff entrance. That should keep the flow of people going."

"There's not going to be enough food," she whispered. "What will we do when it runs out?"

I looked at the long line of people slowly snaking its way through the door. By some miracle, everyone was being orderly, but Freya's fear was justified. In our grand hall, we could seat and feed over a thousand people for a formal banquet, more for a buffet. We could probably handle as many as two thousand, but there were so many more people than that. I waited until my father came to the front of the line before I ventured into the crowd myself.

"We meet again," I said.

He smiled up at me. "This is a nice thing you are doing. There are a lot of hungry people. They need someone to take charge. If I was the Sultan, I'd do the same."

I wanted to tell him that he was the sultan and that the only way I knew to do something like this was from following his lead. He'd made it his life's work to make sure that not one person in the kingdom went hungry. This was his legacy. I wanted to tell him all this, but I couldn't. I wanted to hug him, but I couldn't do that either. I had to let him go. To get his food along with all the others. At least, I knew he was alright, and he was eating. It was all I could hope for right now.

The staff was coming and going almost as fast as the people were filing in. They filled the tables up quickly then turned to head back to the kitchen to grab more. They knew the drill. They might not know my father. They might not even know my mother or me, but they knew how to do this.

I helped, collecting platters as they were emptied

and passing them to the staff to refill. Freya joined in, helping along with most of the palace staff. I'd been letting people walk through for ten minutes or so when a figure appeared at the other end of the grand hall that made my heart soar.

The line was moving smoothly, so I left my place at the door, ignoring my own empty stomach and bounded through the hall that was filling rapidly.

"What's happening?" Genie asked.

"I opened the doors. I'm feeding them."

I waited for the lecture, but it never came. He gave me a smile. "I've never known anyone quite like you."

"So, you remember me?" I asked. My biggest fear was that he'd forget me again. Apparently, my mother had, and I knew, for a fact, my father only remembered me from our meeting the previous week.

"You are not easy to forget, Gaia. How did it go in Urbis?"

I pulled him out of earshot and told him everything I'd learned. It was only when I'd gotten to the end of my story that I remembered the other problem we had. "The Vizier is back. I saw him with my own eyes. He said it was me that defeated him all those years ago."

A blank look came over his eyes. One I knew only too well. How long would it be before I lost him completely too?

I looked down at his wrists. The cuffs were still there. Not only was he losing his memory, I'd soon lose him to the lamp. The lamp that had been hidden for eighteen years since my father threw it out into the desert.

"May I interrupt?"

I turned to find Jamal behind me. His face was set in stone.

"I thought you were with my mother?"

He raised his eyebrows and pointed to the other side of the room. My mother was helping serve the food to the long line of people. She looked so normal, so happy in her role. I missed her so much that seeing her in these lucid moments made it all the worse.

"When I explained the situation, she demanded that she be down here to help. I couldn't stop her without using force."

"You did a good job. Thank you, Jamal."

I ran to her, pulling her into a hug.

"Gaia! Where have you been, my darling?"

Tears streamed down my face. Jamal was wrong. She wasn't completely lost. There was a part of her in there somewhere still. She stroked my hair as I silently sobbed into her shoulder. I could have stayed by her side all day, but a thought popped into my head. If she remembered me, surely she'd remember my father. I left her side and ran past the line of people snaking through, past Jamal, who was now helping along with Freya, and past Genie, who had stayed at his position near the door where people were leaving. I ran down the corridor, running past people with food in their mouths, in their hands, in their pockets, and goodness only knew where else they had stuffed it. Out through the staff entrance and through the grounds to the street. The person I was looking for was gone, having taken his fill. If I'd have known my mother was going to come to help, I'd have kept my father in the palace. I barely got to speak to him, and now he was gone.

I walked back slowly into the palace. The hall was filling up quickly as more people were coming in than going out.

The staff was valiantly trying to keep up with the demands of the people, bringing up platter after platter of food. My mother took platters from the staff, finding space on the long tables. Freya and Jamal did the same. Guards stood at the main doors to the palace, the doors to the hall, and at the gates to the palace grounds, ensuring order was kept.

A surge of hope flooded me. We were coping. People were doing exactly what they were supposed to. Sure, some were taking more than their share, but it was going much better than I expected it to.

My eyes sought out Genie. He stood in his position at the door, smiling at all the people leaving. To an outsider, they would see him as a guard, but he didn't care if people were taking too much food. He knew as well as I did that people had families to feed as well as themselves. He didn't stop a single person leaving, no matter how full their pockets. When he finally did look my way, I offered him a smile. He returned it, making my heart jump. It was bittersweet. Yeah, he remembered me now, but for how long? The only people I could count on remembering me in all this were Jamal and Freya, and currently, Jamal was mad with me. At least, he was doing a good impression of it, purposely keeping out of my way and casting his eyes in the opposite direction when I did glance his way.

Three hours later, and my feet were almost ready to drop off. I'd run up and down from the kitchen so many times; it felt like I'd climbed a mountain. Dropping of the dirty silver platters in the washing up area, I turned to grab some more full ones, only to find the giant kitchen table empty.

"Where's the food?" I asked one of the nearby kitchen staff, a young girl with pink cheeks and a messy bun with strands of hair falling out.

"It's gone."

"All of it?" I asked, running to the cold room. I flung open the door to find all the shelves emptied. There was nothing left at all.

Back upstairs, I ran to the front doors of the palace. The line of people stretched down Kisbu's mains street as far as the eye could see. So many of them. We'd fed a fraction of them. Dashing back inside, I saw the insanity of my decision. I'd not rationed the food. We'd always had enough when we'd put on our parties before. I'd naively thought we'd be fine, that the kitchen's capacity for making food would be enough, if only for this one day. I was wrong. By a long shot.

"Stop!" I shouted, bustling into the main hall. "Just take enough food for you. Don't put food in your pockets."

Jamal strode over to me. "What's going on?"

"The kitchen is out of food."

He sucked in a breath as he took in the scene before him. So far, everyone had shown decorum, but it would only last as long as the food did, and judging by the platters that were emptying fast, it wouldn't be long.

"We need to close the front gates," Jamal asserted.

"There'll be a revolt!"

"So what do you suggest we do, Gaia? Bring them in

and serve them air? What do you think will happen then?"

"I just wish we had more food. Enough to feed everyone."

Suddenly the room began to rumble. I held onto Jamal for fear of falling. My first thought was an earthquake, but when the tables began to fill with food piled high, I realized it was much worse than any earthquake.

Jamal turned toward the mountains of food. "What the...?"

My heart almost stopped when I realized what had happened. "I just did something stupid!" Pulling away from Jamal I ran past the people grabbing for the food and over to Genie. He was slumped on the floor, his face ashen.

"Did you do this?" I asked him.

With a shaky voice, he answered. "Did you wish it?"

"I said I wish, but it was a figure of speech. I didn't mean it."

"But you said the words. You said I wish?"

I nodded. "But I said it to you before, and you asked me if I was sure. I told you it was a figure of speech. Why didn't you ask me this time?"

He shook his head sadly. "I don't have control anymore. I did then."

He held his hands up. The cuffs on his wrists were chained together. He was becoming the slave to magic he once was...And I only had one wish left.

2ND JULY

The first night back in my own bed was fraught with nightmares. The kingdom was now fed, and, for the moment, the people seemed to be happy. But at what cost?

The day, as lovely as it had turned out to be, meant that Genie was down to one wish, and we were once again without food. Not even Genie knew if my wish of food for everyone would cover just the palace and just for that day, or whether the extent of the magic would travel outside of the kingdom, to the people of Kisbu and maybe beyond. We'd postponed the problem, not gotten rid of it. At least, we still had plenty of food left at the palace after yesterday, so none of us would starve, but what would happen when that ran out?

I didn't know. No one did. My mother had had big ideas about speaking to the farmers once again and opening the gates to the city. There'd been so much talk of sustaining and building and doing the right thing by the citizens of Badalah while we were clearing up the platters, but I knew that it wouldn't last. I didn't dare go and visit her this morning. I wanted to keep hold of the wonderful memories we'd made the night before when I could almost believe that things had gone back to normal.

I rolled over in the bed and saw the outline of Asher in the early morning sun. My nighttime rambles had become a thing of the past, but my affinity for my phoenix was unwavering. I walked over to him and gazed out over my terrace as I gave him a quick stroke of his feathers. Looking out over Kisbu, I saw the streets were calm, everything as it should be.

A knock on my door took my attention away.

"Gaia, it's Freya."

She opened the door and stepped in like she had so many times. Helping me get dressed was not her job anymore. She'd been asked by my mother to find her replacement, but what with everything that had happened since then, it had not happened. Not that I cared. I didn't need help to dress anymore.

"Is everything alright?"

She nodded but didn't speak. There was something wrong. "What is it, Freya?"

"My mother came to the palace yesterday."

"I'm sorry I didn't see her. Is she okay?"

Freya brought her hand up to her face and scratched her temple. "She's fine, but she says the magic is strengthening."

I'd felt it myself; I just hadn't wanted to admit it. I'd had to produce flames on my fingers more regularly just to stop from completely going up in an inferno. I'd hoped it was just me, but if Freya's mother was feeling it, it meant others did too.

"The Vizier is back," I said, flopping down on the unmade bed. In all the chaos yesterday, I'd forgotten to tell Freya.

Her hand moved from her temple to cover her mouth.

"He can't be back. He's dead. I know you said that you thought he was back before. Are you sure?"

"I saw him in Urbis. He told me that I defeated him all those years ago."

Freya furrowed her brows and cocked her head to the side. "He died when you were tiny...before you were born even."

I shrugged my shoulders and stood back up. "He *disappeared* around the time I was born. My birth had something to do with it, and it has something to do with all this magic that's circling now. I just don't know what."

"Didn't you find anything out in Urbis? Did you find your brother?"

"I didn't. There was no birth certificate, no adoption certificate, nothing. It's like we don't exist. I'm not sure I only have a brother, either."

Freya's eyes widened again. "What do you mean?"

It was something The Vizier said to me. I didn't really pick up on it at the time, but when he was telling me that I defeated him, he said it was me and my siblings, plural.

"Huh. You have a huge family then?"

I gave a wry smile. "I'm not sure of that, but there may be more like me. More people of magic with golden rings around their eyes. I just wish I knew where they were. I wish I'd have found my birth mother too. I have no idea who or where she is. I ran out of clues, and I ran out of time."

"What about the old lady you saw at your birth? Did you find out about her?"

I nodded sadly. "I did. She was a midwife. She isn't really part of my story apart from the very beginning of it. I found the house where I was born. It was nothing special at all. It was in the poorest area of Urbis, and it belonged to the midwife, not my mother. The next-door neighbor told me he thought she was murdered earlier this year."

Freya's eyes widened. "Maybe The Vizier did it! If he was looking for you, it would make sense."

I shook my head. "He said it was a woman. He said she looked like a witch, but what does a witch really look like?"

"Er, dark hair, long black robes, green skin, pointy hat." She held her hands up to her head to mime the hat.

I laughed. "I think you've been reading too many fairy tales."

I walked past her to the door. "I have to go, sorry. Can you check in on my mother this morning? Make sure she is alright?"

"Where are you going?"

"I need to speak to Genie. I accidentally wished last night. That's why we had so much food. The magic nearly killed him. Just don't let my mother make any big decisions about Kisbu or Badalah. I know we need to open the city gates, but it needs to be done strategically.

I don't think my mother is in a fit state to make any decisions right now."

"Okay, I'll ask Jamal to help me. He's been spending time with her."

I walked through the palace in my pajamas and robe, not caring what the guards thought. This wasn't normal times.

I knocked on Genie's suite door and opened it without waiting for him to answer.

His office was the same as always, impeccably neat with the exception of a couple of books left out on his desk.

A noise came from his private quarters. This time, I knocked and waited. It was one thing to walk into his office, quite another to invade his private space.

"Genie, it's me."

The door opened. He stood there, looking wretched. He had dark circles under his eyes, and his skin was pale. The chains clanked around his wrists.

"Can I come in?" I whispered.

He opened the door wider so I could slip past him.

"I'm sorry I made that wish yesterday. I didn't mean it. I did it without thinking."

Genie walked across the room and sat on one of the couches.

"Don't apologize for what you did, Gaia. Don't ever apologize. You used your wish to help others. I've only ever seen one other person do that before you. Your father."

"You remember him?" I asked, surprised.

He nodded. "There are moments I remember who I am. When I remember who you are. I cling to them, but it's like holding on to sand slipping through my fingers. I can only cherish the moments I do have before they are gone forever."

I sat next to him on the sofa.

"I'll always be here," I whispered.

He held his hand up to my cheek, and I felt the cool metal of the chains upon my chin.

"Sorry," he said, pulling away as I flinched against the cold.

"The chains made me jump," I said, taking his hand in mine. "I can't live with you like this. I won't."

Genie smiled sadly, almost breaking my heart in the process. "What choice do we have?"

"Genie," I said with a firm voice. "I wish for you to be fr..."

I couldn't get the last word out. He'd clamped his hand down on my mouth. I looked into his eyes that were filling with tears.

"Don't do it, Gaia. Don't give up your final wish for me. I'm not worth it."

He slowly lifted his hand away from my mouth.

"If I don't do it, you'll end up becoming enslaved to someone else. Either I never wish for anything again, or I wish for your freedom. There is no alternative."

"I've been a genie for a long time. So long that I don't even remember my real name. I have come to accept my status in life."

"No! I don't accept it. You let my father free you. Why won't you let me?"

"His circumstances were different then. He'd already got what he wanted. He'd won the heart of your mother and we'd defeated The Vizier... You could use your last wish to defeat The Vizier now."

I shook my head. The Vizier had told me himself that Genie hadn't been powerful enough to stop him. It had been my magic or my birth that had done it. I didn't know why and perhaps I never would.

I looked into Genie's eyes. He was so heartbreakingly beautiful, even as haunted as he was with his past.

I took a deep breath and spoke slowly. "I wish for you to..."

This time it wasn't his hand on my mouth. He pushed his lips against mine, crushing them, taking away thoughts of wishes and Viziers. I leaned into him, kissing him back. I parted my lips, tasting him, and like an addict, I couldn't stop, not that I wanted to. I wrapped my arms around him, bringing him closer still until I felt his body against mine through my silk pajama top. The chains jangled between us until I was so close the sound stopped. His lips were demanding, setting my soul on fire, but the heat I was feeling had nothing to do with the magic inside me. It was all from the burning need for this to continue. I kept expecting him to pull away, to tell me he was too old or that it was wrong, but he didn't. I had to pull back to breathe, to make my heart pump again, to see if this was real or if I'd accidentally wished for it, and it was only magic taking over the pair of us. But Genie couldn't make people fall in love. He'd told me once. The hungry look in his eyes was real, not a figment of my imagination or a wish. His eyes were almost imploring as I sucked in air, just inches from his face, one of my hands in his flowing hair, the other between his manacled wrists. It was the mark of a slave, but now, the only slave was me. I was a slave to him, and I knew I'd do anything he wanted because I wanted it too.

He gave me a small smile, barely a curling up of his lips at the edges, but I caught it. We'd done the unthinkable, crossed the line. He'd kissed me, and I'd kissed back.

He opened his mouth to speak, but this time, it was I that stopped him.

"Don't say it," I whispered.

"Don't say what?"

"Don't tell me that this is a mistake." I couldn't bear it.

"If it's a mistake, it's the most beautiful mistake I've ever made." He leaned in again, and this time, I closed my eyes to receive his lips upon mine, but they never came. Instead, his hands rounded my body and tipped it before he pulled me upwards. I opened my eyes to the sounds of the chains clanging beneath me and found that I was in his arms, being carried from the sofa of his living room to the bedroom.

Laying me on the bed was easy, extricating his hands from beneath me less so. The cuffs and the chain tying them together pulled on my pajamas and dug into my skin, so I had to arch my back to let him pull them out. I lay down, staring up at him expectantly, waiting while my burning magic swirled within me, fueled by desire.

He made no move, leaving me confused, unable to interpret what was going on. Then I realized what it was. Any move toward me would have his chains resting on me. I sat up, put my hand on his chest, and pushed slowly until he was lying on his back. He pulled his hands above his head, with the chains going with them. I leaned over and kissed him again, and this time, I let myself fall into what I'd been waiting so long for.

I woke later, a thin sheen of sweat clinging to my naked skin and the warmth of Genie's body against mine. Hours had passed since I'd first come to his room, and the first flush of desire had long since been sated. The only light to touch us was the burning of a torch outside of the room on Genie's terrace, haloing his head, making his hair appear as if it were on fire.

I looked up to find Genie staring down at me. His eyes were warm, alive. I saw something in them I'd not seen for weeks. I saw hope.

I grinned up at him, unable to feel anything but joy, despite the world we were living in and the problems that came with it.

His grin came back, infectious. "You, lady, are something else."

"Is that good or bad?"

"Oh, so good," he said, leaning in and taking my breath away again.

"You don't feel bad about what we did?" I asked once I'd come back up for air.

He shook his head and stroked the skin on my cheeks. The chains jangled lightly as he moved.

"I thought I would. I thought I'd wake up and feel like I'd done something unspeakable. I thought I'd feel shame. I've known you for a long time. That doesn't sit easily on me."

"Do you feel shame?" I asked, propping my head up on my hand with my elbow on the bed.

"I feel nothing but...I can't even describe it. I was once human. Before my enslavement. I thought that part of me was long gone, taken over by the power of magic, but this, what I feel now is power that is much rawer. More real." He twirled a lock of my hair between his fingers and curled up the edges of his mouth. "More wonderful than anything I could ever have imagined, but more than that. It didn't feel wrong. It doesn't feel wrong now. I thought for a long time that if anything happened between us, I would be taking advantage of you."

I leaned forward. "If I remember correctly, it was I that took advantage of you."

He laughed. A loud braying laugh that warmed my heart. It had been a long time since I'd seen him happy. "Yes, you did. You can take advantage of me like that any time you like." He lay his head back on his hands and smirked. I hit him with a pillow.

I could have stayed with Genie, lying in his bed, limbs entangled, tasting his lips until the end of time, but time was something we didn't have. The cuffs around his wrists were proof of that.

"We need to talk about The Vizier," I said, hating myself for even thinking it when I was so happy.

"Who?" Genie replied airily.

I turned to look into his eyes. The cloud had descended again. His memories were once again leaving him.

"Look at me," I demanded.

He flicked his eyes my way, and the genie I knew

returned in an instant. He pulled me close and kissed me.

"Do you remember who you are? How you came to be here?"

It was exhausting, these fleeting lapses in memory followed by even more fleeting returns to normal.

"I don't really know who I am, but I know who you are, and I know how I feel about you. It's probably the only thing I can hold onto. Everything else is fading."

"I need you to hold onto that," I said, taking his hand in mine. Hold onto that feeling, and I'll always be here. Do you remember Aladdin?"

He shook his head. I guess it was too much to hope for. My father had been lost to us the longest.

"A long time ago, he saved you from the lamp. The Vizier I just mentioned wanted to own you. To control you as he had controlled my grandfather. As he had controlled Badalah through my grandfather."

Genie closed his eyes and sucked in a breath through his nose. "I remember. At least I remember feeling unhappy, then happy again. The fabric of my mind is being torn apart."

I kissed him lightly on his temple and whispered. "I know."

"You told me yesterday that The Vizier was back. This man hurt you?"

"Not yet, but he wants to. He believes that I was the one to defeat him the first time. I don't understand it at all, but my birth has something to do with it. I have a brother and maybe more brothers and sisters. Our mother was magic...she had to be, or maybe our father was. We are magic too. I have siblings out there who have magic like mine."

I lit two of my fingers alight and watched the flames flicker in the low light. It diffused some of the pent-up feelings circling inside me. "I think our birth created a burst of magic that defeated all the evil in all the kingdoms. And now it's back along with my magic. Our magic. I wish I knew who my brother was. I could do with speaking to someone about this."

"You have me, my love."

I snuggled up closer to him. "I know I do, but you don't remember how powerful The Vizier is. He's trying to enslave you, and I think he's doing it to get to me."

Genie pulled back. "If that is the case, then I must leave. I cannot put you in danger. I will not play a part in anything that will hurt you."

"You can't leave me. We are bonded with magic, remember? I am the owner of the three wishes, and until I use the last one, you have to be close to me if I want you to be."

"Damn it, Gaia," he said, raising his voice. "Stop this. I don't want to be bound to you because of magic, because I have to be. I want to be bound to you because you want me as much as I want you. I'd use my last breath to keep you safe, but I can't do that if you keep me near you."

He got out of bed and walked backward and forward at the foot of the bed while I sat up and pulled the covers up to my chin.

"I want you. I've always wanted you. What I'm feeling isn't magic. It's so much more than that. Your magic fascinates me, I won't lie, but I loved you before I learned of your magic. I loved you before I knew your magic had returned, and I loved you before I knew of my magic. We are not bonded together because of magic, but because I love you and I hope you love me. But if holding onto that last wish will stop you from doing something stupid, I'll hold onto it. I want you to be free. I've tried wishing it twice now, but both times you've stopped me. I think you did that for a reason. Until I make that last wish or someone finds the lamp, you must always come back to me no matter how far you go."

He sat down on the bed and lowered his head into his hands. "What have I done?"

I moved down the bed, letting the covers fall from my naked body. "Do you love me, Genie?"

He turned his head to the side. "I love you more than I could possibly have imagined. I have spent my entire life not wanting to get close to anyone, but then I fell in love with you. I've tried to fight it. For so long. I love you with everything that I have, which is why you should let me go."

"If you go, I will die. I will have nothing left to live for."

He raised his hands in the air and brought them down over my head and behind my back, bringing me close to him.

"I can't fight The Vizier alone," I whispered. "You were always the person who knew what to do in a crisis, even when you didn't have magic. I want you to be free, but I can't use the last wish anymore. Not until you tell me you'll stay and help me fight."

He looked up. His eyes were red. "I'll fight, and I'll stay with you."

"That's all I want."

I moved to kiss him again, but he leaned back. "I need you to promise me something."

"What?"

"My memory is fading. I slip in and out of the fog. Promise me that you'll save yourself if you need to. Use the last wish to keep yourself safe. Do not waste it on me."

"If your mind goes completely, I promise, but I'm not going to let that happen."

He gave me a sad smile. "And I need you to stay as safe as possible. I know you don't like being cooped up inside the palace, but for now, until we sort this out, I think you should stay inside."

"I promise to stay by you if you promise to stay by me."

His smile came back. "Deal."

He leaned forward and kissed me. We didn't leave his room for the rest of the day or night.

3RD JULY

Genie slept peacefully as I slipped out of bed and pulled on my pajamas for the first time in 24 hours. I kissed him lightly on the cheek and tiptoed across the floor and out through his private suite and into the corridor. Looking both ways to make sure no one noticed me, I ran all the way back to my room and jumped in the shower.

My magic had become almost incontrollable thanks to the high emotion and the lack of letting it out. Igniting my fingers for a few seconds was not enough to diffuse the swirling energy. I let the fire burn as the cold water of the shower hit me with a hiss. I let myself sizzle until my magic was burned out completely, and only then, did I turn the shower up a little warmer and wash my hair. I'd known for a while that my magic was strengthening. That, in itself, was not a problem. If The Vizier's was growing, then having mine strengthen was a bonus, but I needed to learn to keep it under control. I couldn't run to the shower after moments of extreme emotion because now that I was with Genie, strong emotions were going to be a part of my life. Not to mention the emotions that went along with running a kingdom.

I jumped out of the shower and dried quickly. My wonderful day with Genie yesterday had been perfect, but I'd left my mother alone when she needed me the most. I'd left the whole kingdom alone to indulge in my own pleasure.

I dressed in my most business-like attire and left my room to find my mother.

She wasn't in her room, nor in the breakfast parlor, although breakfast had been laid out ready for her. It wasn't the usual breakfast affair, but some bread, butter, and fruit. I picked up a slice of bread and slathered the butter on it thickly. I'd not ventured from Genie's room the whole day before, so our food supply had been limited to the fruit bowl he kept in his bedroom.

I'd been hiding from the world, I realized as I wolfed down the bread and picked up an apple. I'd been using my time with Genie as an excuse not to have to do anything else.

"Nice of you to show up," Jamal said, grabbing a plate.

"I was looking for my mother. I think we need to come up with a plan of what to do now."

Jamal raised his eyebrows and pursed his lips. "If you'd have not spent the whole day in Genie's room, you would know that we already came up with a plan. Your mother is in her study. I said I'd bring up some food for her."

My cheeks colored. So Jamal knew where I had

been. I guessed the rest of the palace did too. I'd never promised Jamal anything, but he'd stayed here in our moment of need for me. I knew that.

"I'm sorry, Jamal."

"Yeah," he said, retreating from the room with the plate of fruit. I ran after him down the corridor.

"What's the plan?"

He didn't stop. If anything, he picked up his pace so that I had to keep running just to keep up with him.

"The gates need to be opened, but tension is high on both sides. Your mother was in talks with people from Kisbu and those from out of the city yesterday."

He turned and began to walk up the main stairwell to the office my mother and father had shared when things were peaceful.

"How did she speak to people from the outside if the gates were closed?" I asked breathlessly.

He finally stopped and turned to face me. "Freya and I took her to the gates yesterday. As the Sultana, she was allowed to pass through. We ventured to the city of Khoha to speak to the mayor there. The mayor agreed to speak to the leaders of the other nearby towns to come up with a plan. I'm surprised you care."

"What do you mean? Of course, I care."

"You didn't seem to care yesterday. I came to find you so you could come along. Freya told me you'd gone to speak to Genie. I assume you stayed there all day because I couldn't find you when I got back either."

There was no point denying it. I wasn't planning to hide my love of Genie. I just hadn't thought I'd have to admit to it so soon. There were so many other things going on that I'd hoped to fly under the radar a little longer.

"I said I was sorry. If you knew I was with Genie, you should have knocked on his door."

"So it's true then? I'd really hoped I was wrong." He moved to turn away from me, but I caught his shoulder.

"You should have come and got me."

"Would you have left his bed for me?"

I was silent. He was right. Nothing beyond the palace being on fire would have dragged me from Genie yesterday.

"I thought so," he said, turning away and walking down the corridor.

My mother was sat in her usual chair in her study. The room only had two chairs. My mother's at one side of a table and my father's at the other. This is the place where they ruled the kingdom together. Freya stood to my mother's side as they both peered down at a piece of paper. They both looked up as Jamal and I entered the room.

"Jamal...and Gaia, darling. It's so lovely to see you. Jamal, what's the matter?"

"Nothing," he said, dropping the plate of fruit onto the table with a thump. An apple rolled out. Freya picked it up and gave me a questioning look.

"Later!" I mouthed at her from behind Jamal's back.

"I think everyone is on the same side," my mother said. "I received this letter from the Mayor of Khoha this morning. She really is a delight. She said that if we open the gates to the city, she will make sure that the farmers bring food. I assured her yesterday that I'll lower my previous tax hike. I don't really know what possessed me to raise taxes in the first place. I've really not been myself these past few weeks."

Jamal rounded the table and sat in my father's chair. Something about it annoyed me, but I kept my mouth shut. I'd never seen anyone sit in my father's chair besides my father. It made no sense for Jamal to stand though when there was a perfectly good chair to sit in, and it wasn't like my father was going to show up any minute now.

"Don't sit there, Jamal darling," my mother said.

Jamal stood up at her request.

"Why not, Mother?" Did she remember Aladdin?

She looked up at me in confusion. "I don't know." She gave a little shiver. "It just feels wrong."

I leaned across the table and looked her in the eyes. "Why? Why does it feel wrong? What is it about that chair?"

Both Jamal and Freya were silent. They knew what I was doing. My father was still in her memory. I just needed to get it out

Tears formed in her eyes. "I don't know. I don't..."

She stood up and walked past Freya and to the door. "Please excuse me."

She bolted from the room, closing the door behind her.

"Well done," Jamal said, his voice dripping with sarcasm.

"She remembers him," I replied, ignoring his tone. "I know she does. Do you know what this means?"

"What?" Freya asked.

"If I can get my father to somehow come to the castle and meet with my mother, she might know who he is again. I can ask the Genie if he can make them fall in love."

I ran from the room, but not before I saw Jamal roll his eyes. Yeah, he was pissed at me for wanting to go and see Genie, but this time it wasn't about me. It was about my parents.

I found him whistling a tune in his office. After our day together yesterday, something had changed in him for the better. His hair was brushed back and tied neatly, and the pallor in his skin was gone.

"Gaia!" he said, pulling me as best he could into a twirl and ending it with a kiss.

"I didn't come to you for that," I said, laughing. On the way there, I wondered if he'd already forgotten our time together. It seemed he hadn't.

"What did you come to me for? Is something wrong?"

He let me go and turned back into the man I knew and fell in love with. This new happy side of him was all kinds of wonderful, but I fell in love with his serious side, with the part of him that could tell me any fact I asked of him.

"I've been thinking about that last wish."

"The one you said you wouldn't use because you don't want to lose me."

I smiled up at him shyly. "That's the one."

He took my hand and pulled me to the sofa. "I've been thinking about that. I won't leave you. Not ever. But I still don't want you to free me. I'm yours whatever you do, but you might need that wish for something more important than me."

I kissed him slowly, inhaling his spicy scent. "There is nothing more important than you."

His eyes crinkled up at the side. "You are more important than me. Keep the wish until you really need it."

"Actually, the wishes are the reason I'm here. What exactly did my father wish for? You can't make people fall in love right, so what did he do to make mother fall in love with him?"

"You are asking me about your father again? You know I don't remember. I only remember being inside the lamp and then living here, being an aide to your mother."

"My father was a brilliant leader," I prompted.

Genie stroked my hand. "I know. You've told me. I know you want me to remember him, but I can't."

"He was only the leader he was because of my mother. They were an inseparable team. They worked so well together, and they were so in love. Even after eighteen years together. I've never known another couple love each other as much as they did."

"They were very lucky to have found each other. Just as I am lucky to have found their daughter."

My mouth turned up at the corners. I wasn't used to him talking this way. It was sweet but funny at the same time.

"If I asked you how you think I could get someone to fall in love with me using wishes, what would you say?"

"I'd say, be you, but I'm guessing that's not what you are really asking."

"Whatever made my parents fall in love before, I'm going to try and recreate it. My father was at the palace

ng you needed to do. I have no doubt that
would have fallen apart these past few
t you being here, but I can see how tired
to deal with The Vizier, and my mother
ıy father comes back to the palace and we
him to stay, maybe he and my mother will
h each other again. Then you can rest."

't move, but Freya took hold of his arm.

We can't let Gaia go alone. It won't be a
ase. We know where he's been sleeping.
is right. You do need a rest. If Aladdin
e can all have a little time to ourselves."

ression softened.

e palace through the staff entrance and
across town to the old bell tower.

t the base of the tower was partially open.

mal said, stepping forward, but I held my
op him.

go up alone."

ed like he was about to argue, but once
ok his arm.

. He's her father. He won't hurt her."

't look particularly happy about it, but I
nd up the stairs before he could think of a
me.

opped the copy of The Badalah Beacon he
nd made to jump out of the window the
fore.

n't!" I said. "I'm here to help you. You
e? From the palace the other day? I'm
daughter of Sultana Jawahir."

the other day. My mother missed him, but if I found him and introduced them, maybe they'll remember each other. I just want to make it the same as the first time. He was a street rat, she was a princess. How did they even meet?"

"Hmm," Genies said, crossing his legs and stroking his chin. "If you were a street rat and wanted to marry a prince, I'd conjure up new clothes. I'd make you look like a princess."

I thought back to how my father looked the last time I saw him. His clothes were filthy and full of holes, and he hadn't shaved in weeks. "I can do that. I have all his clothes here. I just need to get him to the palace under some pretense and get him cleaned up."

Genie shook his head. "You promised me you wouldn't venture outside."

"I promised I wouldn't venture outside alone."

Genie sighed and pulled me close to him. He rested his chin on my head and sighed loudly. "I knew falling in love with you would keep me on my toes."

I felt the corners of my mouth pulling upward and my heart skipping along quickly with the words he'd just spoken. I pulled my head out from under his and kissed him again. This time quickly and with the grin still on my mouth. "I never promised you otherwise."

"No, you didn't," Genie accepted. "So who will you take out with you? Jamal and Freya?"

I cocked my head to the side, surprised. "You wouldn't mind if I went out with Jamal?"

"Jamal is a good man. He's been working hard to keep this place together and with nothing in it for himself. He doesn't wish to take over, nor to overthrow the palace. He has a good heart and a strong head."

"He's completely in love with me," I pointed out.

"All the more reason I trust him. He'd be a fool not to be in love with you. It's all the other men in this kingdom that aren't in love with you that I don't trust. They are all fools."

I pushed his shoulder playfully and let out a laugh. "You are not supposed to say things like that. You are supposed to be consumed with raving jealousy over any man that looks my way."

He leaned forward and kissed my forehead. "My Gaia. I trust you. That is all there is to it."

I wanted to stay, to repeat our day from yesterday, but if I kissed him one more time, I wasn't going to leave his room at all, and I needed to. I had a job to do.

"I'll go and find him. I'll come back and let you know how we fared."

I found Jamal and Freya deep in discussion in the garden. They both looked up as I neared them, but it was Jamal that spoke.

"The Sultana is asleep if you are looking for her. The magic came over her, making her forget what we were doing and gave her a migraine. I thought it best to let her sleep today and worry about opening the gates tomorrow. People are getting fractious again, but I think they can wait one more day."

"Actually, that's a good thing. I have a job I need to do, and I was hoping you'd help me with it. Both of you."

Jamal raised an eyebrow as Freya stood up.

"Anything. What do you want us to do?"

the other day. My mother missed him, but if I found him and introduced them, maybe they'll remember each other. I just want to make it the same as the first time. He was a street rat, she was a princess. How did they even meet?"

"Hmm," Genies said, crossing his legs and stroking his chin. "If you were a street rat and wanted to marry a prince, I'd conjure up new clothes. I'd make you look like a princess."

I thought back to how my father looked the last time I saw him. His clothes were filthy and full of holes, and he hadn't shaved in weeks. "I can do that. I have all his clothes here. I just need to get him to the palace under some pretense and get him cleaned up."

Genie shook his head. "You promised me you wouldn't venture outside."

"I promised I wouldn't venture outside alone."

Genie sighed and pulled me close to him. He rested his chin on my head and sighed loudly. "I knew falling in love with you would keep me on my toes."

I felt the corners of my mouth pulling upward and my heart skipping along quickly with the words he'd just spoken. I pulled my head out from under his and kissed him again. This time quickly and with the grin still on my mouth. "I never promised you otherwise."

"No, you didn't," Genie accepted. "So who will you take out with you? Jamal and Freya?"

I cocked my head to the side, surprised. "You wouldn't mind if I went out with Jamal?"

"Jamal is a good man. He's been working hard to keep this place together and with nothing in it for himself. He doesn't wish to take over, nor to overthrow the palace. He has a good heart and a strong head."

"He's completely in love with me," I pointed out.

"All the more reason I trust him. He'd be a fool not to be in love with you. It's all the other men in this kingdom that aren't in love with you that I don't trust. They are all fools."

I pushed his shoulder playfully and let out a laugh. "You are not supposed to say things like that. You are supposed to be consumed with raving jealousy over any man that looks my way."

He leaned forward and kissed my forehead. "My Gaia. I trust you. That is all there is to it."

I wanted to stay, to repeat our day from yesterday, but if I kissed him one more time, I wasn't going to leave his room at all, and I needed to. I had a job to do.

"I'll go and find him. I'll come back and let you know how we fared."

I found Jamal and Freya deep in discussion in the garden. They both looked up as I neared them, but it was Jamal that spoke.

"The Sultana is asleep if you are looking for her. The magic came over her, making her forget what we were doing and gave her a migraine. I thought it best to let her sleep today and worry about opening the gates tomorrow. People are getting fractious again, but I think they can wait one more day."

"Actually, that's a good thing. I have a job I need to do, and I was hoping you'd help me with it. Both of you."

Jamal raised an eyebrow as Freya stood up.

"Anything. What do you want us to do?"

I glanced at Jamal, who looked at me with a surly expression. Genie was right about him. He made a fine leader. If only he wasn't so angry with me, then I'd feel a lot more comfortable.

"I want to go find my father."

"Again?" Jamal inquired, his voice full of contempt.

"My mother remembered him this morning."

Jamal stood. "She didn't remember him. She merely didn't want me sitting in his seat."

"Right," I agreed, "but she couldn't articulate why. There was no logical reason she didn't want you sitting there. There was a spare chair and three of us standing. It would have made more sense for her to offer one of us the empty seat."

Jamal sighed. "I have enough things to deal with other than go on another wild goose chase around Kisbu. Why not ask Genie to take you since you two are now so cozy?"

"Jamal!" Freya admonished.

I hadn't asked Genie, and he hadn't offered, even though he wanted me to be safe. The reason was his chains. The second he left the palace with his chains on display, the people would see what he'd become again. Some of them wouldn't remember him, but those that did would panic. They'd guess the truth, that The Vizier was back. It would set up a major panic throughout Kisbu and Badalah, making the situation even worse than it already was.

"I'm asking for your help. I want to find him because he was a great leader. You are doing an amazing job of leading this kingdom, Jamal. I've watched how you've taken the reins without asking for anything, and you've done everything you needed to do. I have no doubt that this kingdom would have fallen apart these past few weeks without you being here, but I can see how tired you are. I have to deal with The Vizier, and my mother can't help. If my father comes back to the palace and we can convince him to stay, maybe he and my mother will fall in love with each other again. Then you can rest."

Jamal didn't move, but Freya took hold of his arm.

"Come on. We can't let Gaia go alone. It won't be a wild goose chase. We know where he's been sleeping. Besides, Gaia is right. You do need a rest. If Aladdin comes back, we can all have a little time to ourselves."

Jamal's expression softened.

"Fine."

We left the palace through the staff entrance and made our way across town to the old bell tower.

The door at the base of the tower was partially open.

"I'll go," Jamal said, stepping forward, but I held my hand out to stop him.

"I'd rather go up alone."

Jamal looked like he was about to argue, but once again, Freya took his arm.

"Let her go. He's her father. He won't hurt her."

Jamal didn't look particularly happy about it, but I ran past him and up the stairs before he could think of a reason to stop me.

Aladdin dropped the copy of The Badalah Beacon he was reading and made to jump out of the window the way he had before.

"Please don't!" I said. "I'm here to help you. You remember me? From the palace the other day? I'm Princess Gaia, daughter of Sultana Jawahir."

He nodded, and his demeanor relaxed. "I remember you. Why are you here?"

"I'd like you to meet my mother."

His eyebrows shot up, and he backed up a little. His eyes darted to the window.

"I'd like to take you to the palace and give you some clean clothes and a shave and then introduce you to the Sultana."

"Why? Why are you so interested in me? Why won't you leave me alone?"

"I only want to help you."

"I don't need help."

I looked down at the clothes he was wearing. They were filthy and ripped. He was clean, but his clothes weren't. They were the same clothes he'd left the palace in all those weeks ago.

"If you won't come to the palace, at least, let me buy you some food and a clean outfit."

He wavered then spoke. "You have food?"

I didn't. I'd not thought to bring any. "I don't have food now, but I can bring you some tomorrow."

I looked out of the window at the palace. There was no way I was going to be able to get him to the palace without force, and I didn't want to do that. I needed him to be comfortable when he met my mom for the first time...again. My eyes drifted down to a restaurant on the street. It had a sign saying closed like most of the other restaurants in town. Distribution problems due to the city gates being closed had forced most food businesses to shut. Well, I was going to open them, and I was going to make sure my father was there when I did.

"Come to the window," I said, beckoning him over.

I pointed down to the restaurant that was rather aptly named The Sultan's Shawarma. "Come to the restaurant tomorrow evening, and I'll make sure you get fed."

He didn't answer, but then I didn't expect him to. He was wasting away, though, and the skin was loosening on his bones. He would come. If he'd come to the palace for free food, he'd go to a restaurant.

Back at the palace, I ran straight up to my parents' room and began to rifle through my father's wardrobe. Pushing his ceremonial clothing to one side, I picked out a pair of simple pants and a shirt. I might not be able to get him to wear them, but I could try. I also found some shoes and bundled them all up into a bag, which I dropped off in my room. My next stop was to see my mother. She was having dinner alone in the dining room. She barely registered me as I took a seat next to her. Before I even spoke, I knew she wasn't herself again. The building and fading of the magic exhausted me more than if my mother had lost her memory for good. It gave me hope then pulled it out from under me.

"How are you feeling?" I asked my mother hesitantly as a member of staff brought me a plate of spicy chicken and couscous.

She looked up from her food and stared right through me.

"The headache gone?"

"Mmmm," she answered, going back to her food.

My plan was starting to feel like a colossal waste of time. My father didn't want to go anywhere, and my mother barely knew what day it was, let alone who my father was. All I could do was talk to her and hope she took some of it in.

"I was thinking of taking you to the city gates tomorrow," I began, taking a bite out of the chicken. "You promised that you'd instruct the guards to open them so that people in Kisbu can eat. I thought we could go down after breakfast and help deliver the food."

My mother played with her couscous, moving it around the plate with her fork and not taking a bite. With all the starving people in Kisbu, it pained me to see my mother voluntarily not eating.

After dinner, I helped her to her room and got her ready for bed. She didn't complain, but neither did she say anything else. She was compliant, letting me pull her nightdress over her head. Our roles were reversed. I was no longer the child. It broke my heart to see her like this. She gave me a small smile as I said goodnight to her, but when I returned it, she'd already closed her eyes for sleep.

The pain I felt over my parents intensified and began to burn under my skin.

Wherever The Vizier was, the magic was definitely intensifying. It made me wonder if he was in Badalah. He knew where I lived, and he'd made it pretty clear to me that he blamed me for his previous downfall.

I'd kept my wits about me while I was out in Kisbu earlier, and nothing had happened, but the pressure was building. I could feel the heat seeping out of my pores. Like a schoolboy around a hot girl, cold showers were fast becoming my best friend. I could release all the heat from my body and then cool down afterward. It was annoying, but it was also a necessity.

As the night crept in, I wandered the palace toward Genie's room. There was no point in hiding where I was sleeping. Half of the staff already knew, and the other half had forgotten who either Genie or I was. It made for interesting conversations with guards, who, most of the time, appeared bewildered.

As I passed the open terrace, I glanced out to see Jamal and Freya together. They were just chatting quietly among themselves, but I sensed an intimacy between them I'd not seen before.

I was surprised by the pang of jealousy that reared up within me. I was with the man I loved, and I'd never had true feelings for Jamal, but watching him with my best friend caught me off guard. It felt like I was being left out. It was my own fault, I knew that, but Jamal and Freya were the only two people in Kisbu who hadn't lost parts of their minds.

I pushed the feeling down and carried on walking to Genie's room.

I didn't need any invitation to stay the night.

4TH JULY

Pain shot through my face as my nose hit the floor. The agony and shock of being hurled out of bed with such force caused my body to erupt, setting the covers on fire.

"What's happening?" I screamed, pulling myself to my feet. On the other side of the room, Genie stared at me as though I were a feral creature invading his room. With blood dripping down my face, I picked up a vase and threw the water, flowers, and all into the inferno that the bed had become. It barely made a dent in the flames.

Genie recovered from his shock at finding a girl he didn't know in his bed because that was what had happened. He'd forgotten me again. I saw it in his eyes as he grabbed the flaming covers and tossed the whole lot out of the window. We both watched from his terrace as the covers blazed, then finally settled to the ground in a blackened heap.

"Why are you in my room?" he said, handing me a handkerchief to stem the bleeding.

He wasn't scared of me, even though he didn't recognize me. His throwing me from the bed had been a reaction to the shock of waking to find a stranger in his bed.

Sadness crept into my very soul. He'd forgotten me before, but I'd hoped that after we'd made love, his memory of me would be fixed. It seemed I was wrong.

"You invited me into your bed."

He shook his head as though trying to find the memories trapped inside it.

I kissed his cheek as tears fell down mine. "I'll see you later."

His face showed a look of confusion that broke me to my core. Whatever this magic was or where it was coming from, I needed to stop it.

I threw on a robe, left his room, and ran to my own in bare feet, feeling torn. I had two main problems to deal with. The cause of the magic, namely, The Vizier, and the effect of it, and the people of Kisbu going hungry. I'd been putting too much energy into the latter, thinking if my mother and father met again, the problems would solve themselves. The bigger issue was The Vizier, but I didn't know how to deal with him. He'd not shown himself since attacking me in Urbis. I didn't even know if he was still there or if he'd made it to Badalah. It certainly felt like he was closer, but there had been no sightings of him as far as I knew. I sat on my bed. Asher flew to my lap.

"I'm sorry, Asher. I've not been a good friend lately, have I?"

He gave me a whistle then, opened his wings, and took flight. I watched as he crossed the room and picked something up from the desk on which his perch rested before bringing it back over to me.

He dropped the yellow envelope on my lap and flew out onto the terrace to stretch his wings.

I turned the envelope over in my hands. The return address was stamped on the back. Urbis Central Archives. My heart rate increased as I remembered my request to Derek, the Junior Archivist, who had helped me at the archives. I'd asked him to send me information in a yellow envelope.

With mounting excitement, I ran my finger under the wax seal, breaking it.

Inside, wasn't the birth certificate I'd hoped for, but a number of newspaper clippings and a handwritten note.

I moved the clippings to one side and began to read.

Your highness, I hope this letter finds you well. I'm afraid I haven't found any more information out about your siblings, but I did notice something odd. I don't know if it pertains to your particular query, but I think the top article will bring a smile to your face. Yours sincerely, Derek Waterton, Junior Archivist.

I put the letter to one side and picked up the pile of newspaper clippings. As Derek had predicted, the first one did make me smile. It was an old copy of the Badalah Beacon dated January 14th of the year I was born, or possibly the year after if I was born in December.

It was a photo of my mother and father looking so young. In my mother's arms was a tiny baby. Me.

The headline read 'Royal family welcomes new arrival.'

I read the article underneath. It mentioned I was a surprise to the people of Badalah and that I'd been adopted, but where from was very vague. I guessed that was because my parents had been deliberately vague when interviewed for the article. There were quotes from both my parents saying how delighted they were to have me and how much they loved me already.

I set it aside with the intension of showing it to my mother later. If she saw it, she wouldn't be able to deny that my father existed.

I picked up the next one, surprised to see it wasn't from the Beacon, but from the Draconian Sentinel. The article was remarkably similar to the one I'd just read except it was king and queen of Draconis, our neighboring kingdom, who were the ones smiling down at a small child. The article was almost word for word the same as the one I'd just read. It was as though Princess Azia Rose had just appeared at the Draconis castle one night. The article didn't say that's what had happened, but it also didn't say where she'd come from. It didn't take a big leap of faith to see why Derek had picked this article out for me. I lifted my eyes to the top of the page. The date read January 2nd, the same year as mine.

I put it to one side and found a small clipping next. It wasn't the front page like the others, so I couldn't see which paper it came from, but I didn't need to. It mentioned the king and queen of Floris. There was no mysterious adoption here, but a baby had been left on their doorstep, and they'd decided to take it in. It mentioned that the baby was a boy. I thought back to my knowledge of the royal family in Floris. They had one daughter, no sons. Princess Lilian if memory served. The name caught my attention. Before all this mess had started, I'd read something about Princess Lilian of Floris. I pulled out the stack of newspapers I'd hoarded when I first noticed something going on. I sifted through them until I found what I was looking for. A Copy of the Floris Buckle. I'd been tracking the blight that had overcome the flowers in their kingdom, coming seemingly from nowhere. The last copy I'd picked up had a wedding on the cover. Princess Lilian and the palace's head gardener, Deon.

I read the article with interest. I'd read so many articles from so many kingdoms that a lot of them had blurred together in my mind, but this one had stood out. The wedding had started out between Princess Lilian and Duke Remington, and she'd swapped suitors halfway through and married the gardener. It brought a smile to my face now, just as it had the first time I read it. What a scandal it must have been. And yet she looked so happy in the arms of Deon.

I looked at the small scrap of paper that Derek had sent. The little boy that had been left on the king and queen's doorstep. They'd named him Deon.

My body was abuzz with so much excitement that I had to leave the flammable papers and walk out to the terrace to let some of the excitement out in the form of flames from my fingers. I gave a phoenix call. Asher flew through the flames, weaving between them. The fire didn't bother him at all. I pondered the information I'd found out. Was it possible that Azia and Deon were my brother and sister? I'd seen two babies born in the memory, but I'd walked in halfway through. The Vizier had said siblings. A thought occurred to me. I ran back inside and picked up the old copy of the Floris Buckle with the photo of Princess Lilian and Deon. I studied his eyes. It was hard to tell in a black and white photo, but was it possible that he had a golden ring around his iris too? I searched through the old newspapers until I came upon a copy of the Draconian Sentinel. One more recent than the one announcing Princess Azia's adoption. I pulled one out of the stack and stared at the picture on the cover. It was a photo of Azia's brother lying on the ground with his eyes closed. A man with long white hair leaned over him, and at the very edge of the photo, the princess Azia running into the shot. Her head was slightly to the side, so yet again, I couldn't see her eyes. If only newspapers printed pictures in color and I could have my answer. I'd met some of the royals before. My parents often took me on their royal visits, but I'd never paid attention to the eye colors of the young princes and princesses. Why would I have? My own eyes always had the hint of gold around the iris, but it was only in times of high emotion or intense stress that it really shone out, almost lighting up.

I looked at the remaining snippets cut from newspapers. These were birth announcements. One from Atlantice and one from Enchantia. Both from January, eighteen years ago. There was nothing in them about adoption, but it was a strange coincidence. Five kingdoms, each having a child either born to or adopted by the royals. I needed to find out about the other kingdoms, but first, I needed to sort out the more immediate problem.

Folding the newspaper clippings up carefully, I put them with the huge stack of newspapers I'd already amassed, to look at them later. There was something that linked us all; I just wished I knew what it was. Something that went beyond our births. It was insane to think I might have four brothers and sisters out there, quintuplets. It wasn't beyond the realms of possibility, but it was rare. If, of course, I was right. None of it made sense in my mind. I needed to mull it all over. Normally I'd do my best thinking bouncing ideas off Genie in his office, but I wasn't in a hurry to venture back there today. Him not remembering who I was hurt more than I ever imagined it would. Instead, I was going to do what I'd set out to do before getting the letter from Derek.

I dressed quickly and headed to the breakfast room. I was surprised to find Jamal and Freya there talking with my mother. Her eyes were bright, and she was talking with such animation with them. While Genie's memory had faded again, it seemed hers had come back a little. The whole thing was exhausting, but at least, it would make my plan for today much easier to execute.

"Gaia," Jamal said a smile on his face. "We were just talking about heading to the gates." He nodded his head toward my mother.

It was a relief he was talking to me at all.

"We thought we'd all go after breakfast," he added, pulling out a chair for me. I sat next to him with a little trepidation. He'd been so upset with me. What had changed?

My mother passed me a scone and a plate of butter. "This has gone on long enough. We'll open the gates, travel to Khoha, and ask the mayor to tell the farmers to bring the food."

I gave her a smile. The sooner we got food into Kisbu, the sooner the restaurants could open, and the sooner I could introduce my parents to each other, and then they'd fall in love again. In theory, it sounded so easy. In reality, there were a million reasons it could all go wrong.

We headed into town flanked by a dozen guards. I could sometimes get away with being invisible, but my mother was a different story. People came out of their houses and shops to see what was happening as we walked through the streets to the gates. We could have taken Palanquins or a royal carriage, but my mother insisted we walk among the people. The carriage that would take us to Khoha had been sent ahead of us, to meet us at the gates. I walked a few steps behind her, letting her have all the limelight. The people needed a leader, and she was it. As we walked, our numbers grew and grew, a procession of Kisbu residents following behind us.

The gates of our giant walled city loomed large, making me nervous. I didn't expect food to magically appear at the other side of the gates when they were opened, but the hundreds of people that had followed us were expecting something.

My nerves only increased as my mother ordered the gates open. The whole crowd held a collective breath as the gates were pulled open by four of the wall guards.

A cheer went up among the people as the door creaked to a halt, fully open, exposing the scene on the other side. Almost as many people stood at the other side of the walls as there were on this side, but the difference was, they all carried something. Lines of people, most with carts, some with carriages and the odd one or two with bags strapped to horses and camels, began to walk through the gates.

I turned to one of the guards at the gates. "How long have they been waiting?"

"They started lining up a couple of days ago."

I watched as the farmers and merchants were swamped with people throwing money at them as they began to sell their wares in an impromptu market on both sides of the wall.

All around me, I saw smiling faces as farmers handed over food, and the people of Kisbu gave them money. For a while, it looked like everything was going to be fine after all, but I knew it wouldn't last. The people buying the wares were the people that could afford them. There were plenty that couldn't.

Once the chaos had died down a bit and many of the hundreds of Kisbu residents had gone back to their homes, I climbed a set of steps up to the top of the wall above the open gates. I cleared my throat and shouted down. "Let the farmers be on their way. The gates are open and will remain that way. We need to get food into the shops and restaurants for everyone else."

Okay, it was selfish of me. I needed the Sultan's Shawarma restaurant to open.

The crowd began to disperse as the farmers were allowed through.

"I think this went rather well, don't you?" My mother commented as she handed over a handful of

Rubees to a passing pastry cart. "Cakes for the guards, please."

She picked up four of the delicate little cakes and passed them to Freya, Jamal, and me before biting into the last one herself.

The cakes weren't the freshest. Goodness only knew how long they'd been waiting on the cart, but they were better than nothing, and the guards certainly seemed appreciative of them.

We spent the day walking through Kisbu, as we didn't need to make the trip to Khoha anymore. The sun shone down, lighting the smiles on everyone's faces, and for a while, all was well.

It gave me hope that my plan would work. My mother had never looked so beautiful. As the sun began to lower in the sky, I pulled Jamal and Freya to one side. "I need to find my father. I'll be back in ten minutes."

Jamal nodded and began to steer my mother over to The Sultan's Shawarma Restaurant that was, thankfully, open again.

Pulling my bag firmly over my shoulder, I slipped away from my mother when she wasn't looking and headed up to the bell tower.

My heart fell when I saw that my father wasn't there. I'd brought clothes and shoes for him along with a comb and a bottle of water to clean himself up. I'd even brought a pair of scissors with the intention of giving him a quick haircut. I let the bag fall to the floor, leaving it there. What else could I do? I didn't have the energy to track him down again. I could only suggest he go to the restaurant, I couldn't force him.

With a heavy heart, I ambled back down the dusty

stairwell and crossed the road to the restaurant. Inside, a fuss was being made over my mother. The Sultan's Shawarma, despite the name, was not the kind of establishment that was used to catering to royalty, and it showed. The decor was faded, with wallpaper peeling in places. The menus were covered in grease, and the whole place looked like it needed a good cleaning. The proprietor, a portly man with thinning hair and a thick mustache, seemed to realize the same thing and hastily ran a cloth over the menus as he passed them to us.

We were shown to what I assumed was the best table near the window overlooking the street, and the four of us sat down. Outside, the guards lined up, conspicuous as they were in their palace uniforms.

I leaned over to Freya, who had taken the seat next to me and whispered in her ear. "Can you get rid of the guards? My father won't come if he sees them."

Freya nodded. A few seconds later, she raised her hand to her head and moaned.

"Are you alright, Freya, dear?" My mother asked, full of concern as Freya closed her eyes.

"I'm fine. I think I have a migraine coming on." She opened her eyes and looked over to Jamal.

"Jamal," my mother said, turning his way. "Would you be a dear and take Freya home. Migraines are truly awful. I've been suffering from them myself recently."

"It would be my pleasure." Jamal stood up and held a hand out to Freya. I saw how easily she took it. I watched them through the window as they walked away from the restaurant along with the guards, and he never let go of her.

"I do wish they'd hurry up and take our order," my

mother said, taking me out of my thoughts. "I'm starving. All we've had to eat since breakfast was that little cake from the pastry cart."

My stomach rumbled in answer. As if on cue, the mustachioed man ran over with a bottle of wine and a notebook and pen.

"What can I get you, Your Majesty, Your Highness?"

"I'll have whatever you think is your best dish and lots of it," my mother said, passing him back the menu.

He turned to me to take my order, but then there was a kerfuffle at the door.

"No, no, no," he said to a waitress as she started letting other customers through the door. "The restaurant is closed for a private event," he explained, his eyes darting our way.

We were obviously the private event.

"Don't be silly," my mother shouted over to him. "You've been closed for days. Let them in. The more, the merrier."

The owner wiped the sweat from his brow and ushered them in. The family seemed quite surprised to be eating alongside royalty as they were shown a table near the back of the restaurant.

After I'd ordered, I let my mother dominate the conversation as she talked about how well the day had gone and mulled over ways to carry on the good work. I let her speak. It was nice to hear her thinking again. Every so often, my eyes would dart to the door at the bottom of the bell tower, but by the time our meal arrived, my father hadn't shown.

I started to eat the meal in front of me as my mother talked strategies. I remembered her doing the same thing with my father many times as they debated ways to make Badalah a better place for everyone. It was sad that all their hard work had crashed down in only a few short weeks.

A flash of white took my attention away from my mother. It was my father wearing the shirt I'd brought for him. My heart leapt as he crossed the road and stopped in front of the restaurant. He wavered a little, then when he saw me, he stepped inside.

I jumped up to get him, but he shook his head when he saw me, and his eyes widened. The waitress led him to a table near ours. My plan had been to invite him to our table, but this way was better. He could come over when he was comfortable, and I could think of a way to ease him into the conversation.

"I'll be right back," I said, standing up. "Bathroom break."

My mother nodded and continued to eat as I walked past my father.

"Order what you want," I whispered. "I have it covered."

At the back of the restaurant, I sought out the owner and gave him enough Rubees for my father to have a good meal.

"We never did get to Khoha," my mother said as I sat back down. "I do need to speak to the mayor. The farmers are bringing food in, but it won't last, the way things are. I really could do with having a royal tour, visiting all the main cities in Badalah to turn things around. I just wish I felt better. Every time I make plans, I forget them."

Out of the corner of my eye, I could see my father

listening intently to our conversation. Even when the waiter brought food out to him, he kept looking up at my mother. He was rapt with her. I gave him a smile, but he didn't see it, he was too engrossed with my mother, exactly how I wanted him to be.

I waited for him to make a move and come over. It was plain he was interested in what she had to say as much as he was transfixed by her beauty. They might have forgotten each other on the surface, but underneath, he remembered his love for her. Now I needed him to come to the table and for my mother to see him. So far, she'd not even glanced his way. I was just about to stand up and invite him over when he finished up his meal and stood.

I gave him an encouraging grin as he walked slowly toward our table. He stopped. I held my breath, waiting to see what he would say. He reached down quickly, and when he came up, he had my mother's handbag in his hand. I opened my mouth to question what he was doing, but he ran. Quick as a flash, he was out the door and down the street with my mother's bag.

My mother brought her hand to her neck. "That man stole my bag!"

"Yes, he did," I said with a sigh. My father hadn't stolen anything in his whole life. Why did he have to choose today to start?

The restaurant owner gave chase, but he was nowhere near fit enough to catch my father.

He apologized profusely as I handed him enough Rubees to cover our bill.

Walking back to the palace was particularly fraught. It had seemed like a good idea at the time to dismiss the guards, but as we walked through the streets in the dark, I realized how exposed we were. It wasn't the same as my nighttime trips I'd taken alone. Now, I had my mother to worry about, and she was already nervous after the theft of her purse. It didn't help that the pair of us had dressed in our royal attire to stand out, exactly the opposite of what I'd prefer to be wearing. Only half the town's people recognized me these days and then only half the time, but love her or hate her, they all remembered my mother. They seemed to remember me more if I was around her too. Sometimes like this morning, it brought me comfort, but walking through the dark streets, I'd have preferred to be as incognito as possible.

We finally got home safely, and after leaving her at her room, I went back to mine. My heart ached for Genie, but my soul wouldn't stand a repeat of this morning. Instead, I flopped down on my own bed and wondered why people remembered my mother and not my father.

5TH JULY

"You've never forgotten me, have you, Asher?" I asked as the phoenix flew around the room above my head. The newspaper articles were laid out on my bed around me as I tried to piece everything together. I needed Genie's input. He could see things other people could not. There were so many mysteries. Like who killed the midwife that delivered me? It was a woman, according to her neighbor, and yet the only person I could think that might be an enemy to her would be The Vizier. If he somehow blamed her for my birth or wanted to find me, I could understand that. But it wasn't him. As far as I could tell, the midwife had no money. The house she lived in was in a less than desirable part of Urbis. If only I'd found my mother. I still knew nothing about her beyond what I'd seen in the memory. I didn't even know her name. I picked up the adoption announcement of Princess Azia of Draconis and read it again, trying to glean something more from it.

Copies of the Draconian Sentinel were laid out neatly in chronological order starting from January of this year when I'd started collecting them. My bed looked like a chaos of papers, but there was order there. Just no meaning as far as I could see.

A knock on the door took my attention away from the papers. Freya walked in. Her eyes widened at the mess on my bed.

I handed over a photo of Azia I found from a February edition of the Draconian Sentinel. The accompanying article was about how she'd disappeared, but the photo was from an official photoshoot taken sometime the year before.

"Do you think she looks like me?" I asked.

Freya accepted the paper and squinted. "She has different color skin to you," she said, pointing out the obvious.

"Yes. I know. Look beyond that. Do you see any resemblance?" I took the paper back and held the photo next to my own face. Freya's eyes darted between the two.

"Not really. You are both a similar age and both beautiful, but I don't really see much resemblance. Why?"

I moved a stack of papers and sat back down on the bed. "I think she's my sister."

Freya furrowed her eyebrows and took the paper back from me. "What makes you think that?"

"Look at her eyes. I know it's a black and white photo, but don't you think that bit of lightness around the iris might be golden?"

Freya shrugged, unconvinced. "I'm sorry. I don't see it. What is all this?"

I looked at the piles of papers and felt defeated. My kingdom was falling to pieces, my parents were sick, and I was no closer to finding out what was going on in all this. And the only person that might be able to see the connection didn't even know who I was, despite the fact he'd seen me naked.

Some of the kingdoms' royal families also had babies around the time I was born. Some were adopted in weird circumstances. Some were apparently born to the royals.

Freya picked up a copy of The Conch, Atlantice's daily paper, and read the headline to herself.

"Do you think Princess Blaise is related to you, too?" she asked.

I shrugged. "I don't know. I thought so, but she looks even less like me than Azia does."

Freya walked over to my vanity unit, picked up the chair at it, and brought it over to the bed where she sat it down in front of me. "Walk me through this. You think you are related to what...four other royals? Which ones?"

It sounded so stupid to say it out loud. I had no brothers and sisters, and here I was thinking I was one of a set of quintuplets, none of which looked like me.

"Azia from Draconis, Blaise from Atlantice, Deon from Floris, although he wasn't a royal. He married the princess there a couple of months ago. And finally, Kelis from Enchantia. Before you ask, no, none of them look like me, they just all appeared at their palaces and castles in a similar time frame."

"Weird," Freya said, picking up another paper. "These princes and princesses. Are they in the same kingdoms that have had the problems?"

"Oh, the gods! Freya!" I jumped up and kissed her cheek. "Why did I not think of this?"

I started to rearrange the piles of papers into a makeshift timeline with the photos of the princes and princesses on the top.

"Draconis was first!" I said, pointing to the photo of Azia, my voice full of excitement.

Freya held out a hand. "Wait!" she ran over to my nightstand and brought out a pad of paper and a pen. "Draconis first. What dates?"

I cast my mind back to everything I'd read. "There were problems with the dragons in January. I think it was about that time that the Queen fell asleep, She's not woken up yet."

Freya wrote furiously. "Draconis, Azia, Sleepy Queen, and dragons in January. Then what?"

I looked over at my carefully curated piles of papers. "Princess Blaise of Atlantice. Her mother turned back into a mermaid. That was in late January or early February."

"Blaise, mother a mermaid, Feb. Got it. Next?"

"There was a bit of a gap and then Floris. Now, the princess there is called Lilian, and she's of a similar age, but not quite. It seems the Royals took on a baby boy that year, and he's the one that I think is my brother. His name is Deon."

"Deon. What happened to him?"

"It wasn't just him," I said, picking up a copy of the Floris Buckle with a picture of the royal gardens on the front. All the plants were dead or dying. It was a pitiful sight. "The whole kingdom is a mess. They had a blight on their plants. Everything died."

Freya screwed up her face and wrote some more.

"This was late Feb, early March."

Freya nodded. "Next?"

"The next kingdom I noticed to have problems was The Vale. Then it was..." I checked the pile of papers again. "Arboria."

"And do either of those places have a prince or princess the same age as you?"

I shook my head. "I don't know. The royals from The Vale had a daughter, but I thought she was older than me. She was married and had a baby. The baby was kidnapped."

Freya raised an eyebrow. "You *think* she's older than you?"

I'd never visited The Vale, but I knew the king and queen had a daughter and a granddaughter. They'd endured so much tragedy. First, the husband of the princess had died when the princess was pregnant, and then, the newborn had been kidnapped. My heart hurt just thinking about it. "I don't know. I feel way too young to be married with a child."

"Doesn't mean she is, though, does it? Do you know her name?"

"Eliana."

Freya wrote it down. "Have you noticed that all these names run in alphabetical order starting from A? Azia, Blaise, Deon, Eliana. If you tell me that the prince or princess from Arboria is called Fred or Felicity, then this will be something huge."

"Fallon!" I said, my eyes widening. "And then me."

"Gaia!" Freya mouthed breathily.

We stared at each other open-mouthed as I tried to consider the implications. There weren't just five, there were more.

"The last one I was going to tell you about is Princess Kelis of Enchantia, but nothing has happened there as far as I know. The Enchantia Charm is reporting nothing strange."

Freya picked up a copy of The Charm and read the headline on the cover. It was an article about a mage rescuing a puppy from a burning building.

"Hmmmm. I wonder if the magic hasn't hit Enchantia yet?" she shrugged and threw the newspaper back on the bed. "It's hopping from kingdom to kingdom. Maybe this is more widespread than you think. What if it's happening in all the kingdoms, some of which it hasn't started in yet?"

"So we are missing the letters C, H, I and J...Maybe L, M, N..." she continued. "We are missing the kingdoms Arcadia, Elder, Oz, The Forge, and Skyla. What do you know about the royal families from those places?"

"My knowledge of Elder is limited. They don't have a royal family, and they don't have a newspaper. I know that Skyla is without a royal family too. They kind of live communally, and I'm not even sure who is in charge there."

"What about Arcadia?"

I sat forward. "Arcadia hasn't had any problems as far as I'm aware, and the king and queen are childless."

Freya stood back up. "Maybe we are clutching at

straws then, and the names of the royal princes and princesses are just coincidental."

"Maybe," I mused. "But I don't like coincidences. My mother would probably know more about the leaders of Elder and Skyla. I do know the president of the Forge is called Alice. She has two daughters, Ivy and Pearl."

"There's your letter I," Freya pointed out.

I stood up and followed her out onto the terrace. Asher flew over our heads and out over the streets of Kisbu. I envied him sometimes, the freedom he had to go wherever he pleased. I'd fly to Skyla and Arcadia and all the other places and find out what was going on. If Ivy was part of this, did that mean Pearl was too? If so, where were the other letters of the alphabet? I counted the letters from A to K on my fingers. K was the eleventh letter of the alphabet. Was Kelis the last one, or was Pearl? Eleven children in one go was impossible. I didn't even bother to count to P. Instead of this making sense, it had only thrown more mysteries my way.

I leaned on the balustrade and brought my hand up to my temple. "I feel like my head is spinning."

Beside me, Freya smirked. "I know what you mean. Maybe we should come back to this later. How did it go with your mother and father last night?. Did they meet and fall in love again?"

I almost laughed. "Not quite. My father came to the restaurant and stole my mother's purse."

Freya's eyes widened. "He did what?"

"I was stupid to think that my plan would work. It feels like no matter what I do, it goes wrong. I feel like I'm making everything worse."

"Aladdin isn't a thief. He might have forgotten who

he is, but deep down he's still the same person. He wouldn't steal."

I shrugged. "I saw him do it. He might be the same person, but his circumstances have changed. He's living on the streets. He's hungry."

Freya took my hands and turned me to face her. "You were in a restaurant. I'm assuming you paid for his meal. He didn't steal your mother's handbag because he was hungry. I think you should go and find him and ask him what he was doing."

I sighed and headed back inside. Going to find my father was just another job to add to my list.

"I wish I could ask Genie about all this," I said, indicating the papers still strewn all over my bed.

"Actually, that's why I came to see you. I feel like we've not had a proper talk in ages. What's happening with you and Genie?"

"I slept with him."

Freya grinned. "I guessed."

She quickly moved the newspapers away as I sat back down on the bed. I watched as she stacked them all carefully into one big pile and then placed them by the side of the bed.

She joined me on the bed. "What happened? I thought that he said he was too old for you?"

My heart wrenched as I remembered the way he'd looked at me as I last left his room.

"It was magical, beautiful. I love him."

Freya pulled me into a hug as I tried to keep the tears at bay. I'd always felt so confident in every aspect of my life, and now, there wasn't a single part of it that I felt as if I knew what I was doing.

My foundations had been pulled out from beneath me.

"Does he not love you back?"

I stood up and headed to my bedroom door. "Sometimes, he does. The last time I saw him, he threw me out of his room because he didn't even know who I was."

Comprehension dawned on Freya's face. "Oh, honey. I'm so sorry."

"It's fine. It's not like I'm not used to it by now. First, my father, then my mother, now Genie."

I opened the door and headed out into the corridor. Freya followed.

"Go and have some breakfast," she ordered. "I'll find Jamal, and we can come up with a plan."

"A plan for what?" I asked. There were so many things going on. I didn't know which to prioritize.

Freya smiled. "Everything. We'll break it all down and tackle one thing at a time."

My mother looked up as I entered the breakfast room.

"Gaia Darling. I was hoping to see you this morning. First reports are in. The townsfolk are behaving. The out of towners are still bringing in their wares. It seems things are back to some normality."

I gave her a smile, wishing that were the case. Normality wasn't going to come back just because we opened the gates. The magic had been coming in waves, ebbing and flowing. She remembered me now, but how long would it last?

"I was thinking of heading into town and seeing if I can find the man who stole your purse yesterday," I said airily, slathering butter on a pastry.

"The man needs locking up. I don't want you going to look for him. There's no telling what he might do to you."

I poured black coffee into a cup and took a sip. "He's not dangerous, Mother."

She pointed a butter knife at me as she talked. "You can't possibly know that. I have enough on my plate to deal with without wondering what happened to my daughter if you don't come home."

"Oh?" I said, taking a bite from the flaky pastry. "What are your plans?"

Letting my mother do anything without supervision these days was much more dangerous than looking for my father in Kisbu. At some point in the past few weeks, I'd become a mother to a bunch of toddlers, or at least, that's what it felt like.

"I was thinking of visiting Khoha. I should have gone there yesterday, but of course, I didn't."

Ten minutes later, Freya and Jamal showed up. I watched my mother as Jamal took a seat next to her, but her eyes didn't even flicker toward him. Maybe she was getting better.

"Freya tells me you wanted to speak to me," Jamal said, filling his plate with meats and cheeses.

I glanced Freya's way.

"I was thinking about the current situation with the townsfolk." She turned to my mother. "Your Majesty. I believe you were thinking of visiting Khoha today? The mayor was expecting a visit."

"Was I?" My mother looked surprised. The blankness had descended over her eyes again. It was as if she'd not just mentioned it to me only moments ago.

"Yes. I was thinking that Jamal and I could go with you and help out. I believe Gaia has things to do here."

Jamal looked my way and narrowed his eyes. "Something to do with Genie, no doubt....ow!" He looked over at Freya, who smiled innocently at him as he bent down to rub his leg.

"Actually, I was planning to go into Kisbu and see if I can find the thief that stole my mother's purse."

Now, Jamal looked confused. Freya obviously hadn't told him what had happened with my father the previous day. My mother continued to stare blankly at her plate. At least, I wouldn't have to worry about her stopping me from going out to find my father.

"I'll tell you all about it later," Freya said, motioning toward my mother with her eyes. "How about we all meet back here later and have a debrief?"

Despite how Jamal felt about me right now, I was blessed to have him and Freya here at the palace. Without the pair of them, the whole of Badalah would have collapsed long before now.

An hour later and I was out on the streets of Kisbu, dressed in the same clothes I wore in Urbis. Today I wanted to be able to walk through the streets unseen. I found my father exactly where I expected to find him, asleep in the top of the old bell tower.

I nudged him with my toe and waited for him to wake. He snorted, then opened his eyes, and pulled himself back into almost an attack stance. When he saw it was me, he relaxed.

"I'm sorry about yesterday," he said, pulling something out from under a pile of newspapers. It was my mother's purse. He held it out at arm's length as if it would bite him.

I took the purse and looked inside. All the Rubees my mother had taken out with her were still there along with everything else she usually carried with her.

"I didn't take the money."

"Why did you steal it?" I asked, sitting on the window ledge.

He licked his lips and sat down. "I don't want your money. I don't need it," he reiterated.

I looked around the messy room where he lived with broken floorboards and old newspapers as a bed. "I beg to differ, but if you weren't planning on using the money, why steal it in the first place?"

He ran his hands through his filthy hair. I noticed that he was still wearing the shirt and pants I'd brought for him to wear. I couldn't see his old clothes anywhere.

"The second I saw her, I felt something. I don't even know what. It sounds crazy. I don't even know her. I guess it's because she's the queen or because she's so beautiful. I wanted to come and talk to her. It was stupid, but I thought if I took the purse, I could come to the palace and use it as an excuse to speak to her."

"So, why didn't you? That's why I invited you to the restaurant in the first place."

He raised an eyebrow and narrowed his eyes. I'd forgotten for a second that I'd told him I'd invited him because I wanted to feed him. I'd not even mentioned my mother being there to him.

"I couldn't. Look at me. I'm a pauper, a nothing. Why would the queen want to speak to someone like me?"

I sighed. "My mother would sit and listen to you talk for hours. There was nothing she liked more than to discuss current affairs with you. She just doesn't remember it, and neither do you. You love her. You've been in love with her from the first moment you laid eyes on her and she with you. I've never known any couple more suited to each other than the pair of you. I can't believe you've forgotten everything you had together."

I was shouting, and I knew it. He stared at me, his eyes wide open.

"She's in love with me? The Sultana of Badalah is in love with me?"

"Yes!" I replied exasperated. "She needs you, and you need her. Badalah needs both of you, and so do I."

He closed his eyes and brought his hands up to his temples. "I remember...I remember my childhood. I lived on these streets. How would I know the Sultana?"

I moved from the windowsill and sat next to him on the floor.

"You found a lamp. Many years ago. It contained a genie. The genie helped you meet her. The genie can't help you anymore, but I can."

"You can introduce me to the Sultana?"

"Ye..." I remembered what my mother had told me that morning at breakfast. The second my father set foot in the palace, my mother would have him arrested for theft. "If you truly want to meet my mother, I'll find a way," I promised him. I kissed his cheek and pulled some Rubees from the purse, which I handed over to him. "Get yourself a haircut and some food. I'll do the rest. I'll come back when I've figured out how to play this. Don't go far."

His eyes drifted to the riches in his hands and then to me in amazement. I'd given him enough money to feed himself for a few days and to get himself cleaned up. To me, it was pennies; to him, it was a great deal of wealth. I wished I could give him more.

Back at the palace, I resisted the urge to go and check on Genie. Instead, I went down to the basement to practice my magic while I waited for Jamal, Freya, and my mother to come back. As the Sultana's daughter, it should have been me heading to Khoha with my mother, but I trusted Jamal and Freya. They understood the importance of keeping relations with our nearest town outside of Kisbu cordial. When this was all over, I'd make sure that Jamal had a place in the palace for as long as he wanted. He deserved it.

The fire began to build up within me, almost shooting out of my fingertips as my mind wandered to The Vizier. I reigned it in and kept control of the swirling mass of hot magic within me. In the far corner of the cellar, stood a seamstress's mannequin that had been brought down here when it was no longer needed. Picturing The Vizier's face on top of the feminine body, I hurled my fire at it, sending it flying into the wall in an inferno. It fell to the floor as flames licked the wall next to it.

I'd started the fire, but could I put it out using magic? I didn't know. Imagining a magical lasso, I wrapped it around the flames and began to pull back. The flames pulled away from the wall and the smoldering mannequin and floated in mid-air toward me in a long line as though an invisible rope was burning.

"Cool!" I whispered, waving my hand and letting go

of the magic. With nothing to burn and no magic tethering it to anything, the flames vanished. All that was left were scorch marks on the wall and the blackened mannequin along with the smell of burning.

Later, Freya and Jamal came to find me. The three of us walked out into the gardens away from the guards.

"How did it go?" Freya and I asked simultaneously.

"Your mother forgot who she was," Jamal answered. "We had to leave her in the carriage while we spoke to the Mayor of Khoha."

It broke my heart, but it was no more than I expected, I'd seen the blackness glaze her eyes this morning at breakfast. I'd hoped that once she was out of Kisbu, she'd come back, but it wasn't to be.

"The mayor knows the situation. We told her everything."

"We told her about Aladdin and The Vizier," added Freya

I nodded. No point keeping quiet about it. Not to the mayor, at least. However, I wouldn't like The Vizier's comeback becoming common knowledge.

"And?" I prompted.

"She doesn't remember Aladdin or The Vizier," Jamal said, "but she says that she's noticed a lot of weird things happening. A lot of the people of Khoha have forgotten her too. I think as long as we keep the taxes low for now, she'll do her best. It was all we could ask."

I held my hand out to him. "You did a great job. Thank you." I glanced across at Freya. Her face had taken a sour turn, and I understood why. I'd reached out for Jamal's hand without thinking. I held my other hand toward her, and she brightened up immediately.

"My father stole the purse because he wanted to bring it back to the palace to meet my mother. He wants to meet her as much as I want him to. Unfortunately, I don't think my mother wants to speak to him."

Freya gave an exaggerated yawn. "Maybe we should solve that problem another day?"

I nodded and walked away. When they thought I'd gone, I turned back, and I saw Freya and Jamal kissing. That's why she wanted me to go. She wanted to be alone with Jamal. My lips curled up at the corners as I turned and headed for bed.

6TH JULY

After another night of tossing and turning, I could stand it no more.

My heart ached for Genie. I needed to see him even if he didn't know who I was. My heart pounded as I walked down the corridor that would take me to his suite. As I held my hand up to knock on his door, I hesitated, wondering if I'd be strong enough to have him look at me blankly the way my mother did so often these days. My father remembered me perfectly from all the times I'd visited him since he lost his memories in the first place but nothing from before. My mother's memories flitted in and out, but she seemed to be losing new memories as well as old ones. The magic did not treat people equally. Same with the guards. Some remembered me; some looked at me blankly as I passed them. I was yet to have one try to throw me out because he or she didn't know who I was, but I knew it could happen. And then, there was Genie. Just like my mother, his memories came and went, and like her, his personality had changed. My mother made bad decisions about what to do with the kingdom. Was Genie making bad decisions about being with me? Was his love for me nothing more than a by-product of the evil magic swirling around all of us? Part of me wanted to think that like too much alcohol, the magic was just bringing out everyone's true self, and Genie loved me all the time, but it didn't ring true for my mother. Her decision to increase taxes had almost crippled Kisbu. I was still pondering such things when the door opened.

My fears vanished when Genie pulled me into his arms and swept me into a kiss.

I clung to him as he pulled me inside, our lips still locked together as he managed to close the door behind us with his foot. I kissed back with such fervor, scared that this would slip away and be pulled out from beneath my feet as everything so often had. I held everything close to me, locking it away in my memory. The way he tasted, the light spice on his skin and the way he held me tightly, the chains around my back. And I left mental fingerprints, everywhere I touched, his skin, his hair, his face, terrified that this might be the last time we did this.

He picked me up and carried me through his living room into his bedroom where we made love. What had started off as something fast and desperate became a long, drawn-out dance of making memories for him and for me.

When it was over, I wouldn't let him sleep for fear that sleep would bring back the blank look in his eyes again.

He stroked the side of my face. "There is something very wrong. I can see it in your eyes."

I blinked and sucked in a breath. "The last time I was in this bed with you, you threw me out of it. You didn't know who I was."

He swallowed, and pain clouded his features.

"I am so sorry, my Gaia. I'd wondered why you hadn't visited me for a few days. I wanted to come to you, but the guards don't recognize me anymore. I had to wait for you to come to me. I can't believe I did such a thing."

"I didn't come to you because I was scared you wouldn't remember me. I didn't think I could bear it."

He pulled me to his chest and stroked my hair.

"I have no control over what is happening to my mind. I hate that it is so. Look at me."

I pulled back and gazed into his eyes. It felt like I was looking into forever.

"If I ever forget you again, look at me like this. Exactly as you are looking at me now. I see so much love in your eyes. I will know it in my heart, even if I don't see it in my mind."

I gave him a small, sad smile. "Your mind is what I fell in love with."

"I will always be here, and I'll always keep you in both my mind and heart. If the darkness comes again, know that like the seasons, it will pass."

I laid my head back on the pillow and stared up at the ceiling. "Will it pass? Really? You can't possibly know that. You don't know what this is any more than I do. Most of your memories of the past are warped or gone completely. Freya and I noticed something weird about the princes and princesses of the other kingdoms, but I don't see how it helps us solve the problems we are having here."

"What did you notice?"

I told him everything Freya and I had talked about the previous day. I wished I had all the newspapers to show him, but getting them would involve leaving his bed, something I wasn't ready to do just yet, even temporarily.

He didn't say a word as I talked, but I noticed he watched my lips. If anyone could make sense of what was happening, it was Genie.

"Siblings seem like a stretch when you take into consideration the numbers of people involved," Genie concluded.

"That's what I thought, too, but I saw my birth."

"You saw your birth?"

"I asked you to show you my birth," I reminded him.

He nodded and pulled his hands up and rested his head on them, the length of chain running under his neck.

"I don't think that what happened eighteen years ago is our main priority, even if it does pertain to what's happening now. Perhaps we should put the why's of this on the back burner and concentrate on our more immediate problems."

"Which one? There are so many problems; I don't know what to deal with first."

"List them."

I thought of all the things that were going wrong. Everything seemed the most immediate problem.

"My mother is losing her mind. The city...the whole

kingdom is barely hanging on by a thread. Jamal and Freya are doing a magnificent job, but they are not royalty. I think the only reason that people are accepting them is because everyone's memories are messed up, and no one knows who is who these days."

"Okay, what else?"

"The Vizier. I know he's back because I saw him, but I don't know if he's in Badalah or still in Urbis. He wants to destroy me. He also wants to destroy you, which brings me to problem number three." I pulled on his arm and held up the chain that held his wrists together. "I know how to solve this problem if only you'd let me."

He shook his head. "Not yet. Now is not the time. Is that everything?"

I looked at him incredulously. "Isn't that enough? No one remembers me. You might forget me any second, and I'm scared. What if this becomes permanent, and Jamal, Freya, and I are the only ones that remember anything? What if I lose you, but this time forever? If someone finds the lamp, you'll become theirs. If you forget me, it will be like I don't exist."

"Gaia. You will exist with or without me. Do not base your worth on whether I remember you or not."

"If you don't remember me, I'll have nothing left."

"You've just told me the priority. We need to find a way to make our memories return. Have you looked in my books?"

Genie had thousands of books. His office had bookshelves bursting with them, and there were thousands more I'd not looked at in his living room. We didn't have a library in the palace because we didn't need one.

Genie had enough books to fill two libraries, and every single one of them was nonfiction.

"You don't have any books on magic," I reminded him.

He sat up and brought his hands to his lap. "Not everything has to be about magic. While it is true I have no books on spells or the art of magic, there are other ways to bring back memories."

"What do you mean?"

"Potions have been known to do things that spells cannot. I have told you before that I cannot make people fall in love, but love potions exist. I don't know how well they work, but they are bought and sold in some kingdoms. I suggest you look at books on the other kingdoms to see if you can find anything. My personal library in my living room has books that might help. I suggest you start with The Forge."

"What are you going to do?" I asked as I pulled my clothes back on.

A grin split his face, "I'm going to sleep. You've fair worn me out."

I left him to sleep with a grin of my own. If he forgot me when he woke up, I'd do something to remind him who I was.

Second, only to Genie himself, his magnificent library was one reason I loved being in his private suite. I'd never known the existence of it before that first time he brought me in here, but ever since I knew of it, I'd been dying to search the shelves to read everything there was to read. Of course, that would take me weeks, if not months, and I didn't have that kind of time, so I began my search more methodically. It seemed Genie had cultivated an interest in the other kingdoms, and a quick search showed that the books were organized by region rather than alphabetically by author. Thirteen bookcases, twelve kingdoms, and Urbis.

Instead of taking Genie's advice, I first went to the bookcase with books about Badalah.

The entire history of my kingdom was laid out before me. The books on the very top were old, the spines faded by years of sunlight, their bindings falling apart. Lower down were the newer books. Next to a tourist book on the cafes of Badalah was a hand-drawn book, barely more than ten pages long. I pulled it out and flicked through it, my heart swelling with memories. I'd made this book when I was five or six years old and presented it to Genie. It was the story of a princess in the Badalah palace. Not so original, but the cute scribbles and misspelled words brought a smile to my face. He'd kept it all these years, giving it space among the books of Badalah's history.

Putting it back, I moved to books about The Forge. Just like the ones about Badalah, these books were arranged in much the same way with the older ones at the top and the newer ones at the bottom. Apart from that, there seemed to be no particular order. History books were mingled in with tour guides, fashion guides, and the history of the vampires that lived there.

I could have spent many happy hours finding out about The Forge, but I needed to figure out how to solve the problems of Badalah before I did a spot of light reading for pleasure. With great reluctance, I put back the book of weird inventions I'd picked up and searched for a book on potions. My eyes fell on a shelf that just so happened to be full of books about elixirs and potions. The majority of them were beauty-related, which made me chuckle. I pulled out a book titled The Forge: a kingdom of Technology and Alchemy. The thick tome was so heavy that I had to carry it through to Genie's office and set it on his table to read it. Like many of the other books, this one also made mention of beauty, but it read like a guide to The Forge rather than a recipe book. Pages upon pages were filled with the history of the Red Queen, who although cruel with a penchant for chopping people's heads off, was a true groundbreaker when it came to technology. She ruled The Forge from her house in the capital city of Melfall with the help of mechanical playing cards. The cards were monoliths of size and advanced technology and would roam the streets doing her bidding. The whole thing was fascinating, and I found myself sucked into this weird and wonderful world that was so unlike my own kingdom.

It was only when Genie appeared a couple of hours later and kissed my cheek that I realized I'd been so consumed by The Forge that I'd completely forgotten to look for something that might help.

"What are you reading?" Genie asked, passing me an apple from the fruit bowl in his bedroom.

"Did you know that The Forge has guilds for inventors?" I asked, full of enthusiasm.

"There are many guilds in The Forge. Inventing is just one, although all are art or technology based. The Forge is a strange place. They covet beauty over all else. Their currency is based on it, and yet they have some of the most intelligent minds in all the kingdoms. I once thought I'd like to visit there, but I have always been indebted to your father."

"You remember him now?" I asked, glancing up from the book.

He put his hand on my shoulder. "A little. I had a dream about him. I don't think I'd recognize him if I saw him."

"I'm surprised you stayed here out of a sense of duty. You could have visited."

He nodded his head. "I should have. There was always so much to do here."

I turned my whole body his way. "Why don't we go? Both of us? I could look for someone who could make us a memory potion, and you could finally see the place. We could go to Melfall. It will give me a great excuse to meet Ivy and Pearl, the daughters of President Alice and see if either of them has a gold ring around her irises."

He took my hands in his. "There is nothing I'd like more than to travel with you. Maybe when this is all over, we can travel together and see all the kingdoms, but now..." he shook his head.

"Why not now?"

He held his hands up, reminding me of his bondage to the palace. It wasn't just to me that he was bonded. The second he stepped outside, the people would see him for the slave he was. Many people over the years had looked for the lamp, and none had found it, but it felt like we were closer than ever to someone finding it and using it. Images of The Vizier came into my mind. If anyone found it, I knew it would be him. My father had told me that The Vizier spent years and years looking for it before he'd thrown my father into a mysterious cave in the desert where my father had survived by the skin of his teeth.

"There is one way I know to make these chains go away," I said, wrapping my fingers around the cuffs. I looked up into his eyes, pleading with him. He knew I could wish it all away. If I did it without his permission, he'd still be bound to do what I wished, but to do that, even to free him would hurt him. Not just physically. The actual pain of the magic would pass with a good night's sleep, but to make him do something against his will would put something between us. I wasn't sure if he would ever forgive me, so I had to wait until the stubborn ass changed his mind before I could use my last wish to free him.

"You know I can't let you do that," he said, leaning forward and kissing me lightly on the mouth. My heart skipped a beat at the gentleness of his touch.

"I have lived a thousand lives. You have lived but one, and you are still young. I will not give up your life for my freedom."

The tingle of tears made me blink. "I'm not asking you to save my life. My life isn't in danger right now."

"Gaia..."

He knew the situation enough to know that I was lying to him. My life was in grave danger. Just because that danger hadn't presented itself yet beyond giving me a warning, didn't mean it wouldn't come. The Vizier knew who I was, and he knew where I lived. I was actually surprised he hadn't made himself known here in Badalah yet. I'd instructed the guards to keep an eye out for him, but with half of them not knowing who I was and the other half not remembering who The Vizier was, our protection was at our leanest in years, and that was with a full contingent of guards. The only two people I could trust in all of this were Jamal and Freya. A maid and a farmer, neither of whom had any royal blood, were practically running the whole kingdom. I couldn't expect them to save me from The Vizier, should he decide to appear. They wouldn't be able to. If he did decide to come to kill me, I only had myself and my magic. It would stave him off for a while, but I wasn't powerful enough to keep him away forever. It didn't look good whichever way I looked at it.

"Okay, okay, I know. I won't do it. You know how I feel. I want you to be free. I don't want to accidentally wish for something like I did before and waste it on something stupid. Saying I wish is a turn of phrase that people say all the time."

"I trust you."

I smiled. He had more faith in me than I did in myself.

"I should go. I've left the kingdom to Jamal and Freya long enough. The kingdom needs a leader, and that leader should be me."

"Don't be too hard on yourself. The people of the kingdom don't know what they want anymore. You are doing your best in a strange situation."

I stood and let go of his hands. "I know, but it feels like no matter what I do, it's wrong. The kingdom is still failing, I don't understand what part I have to play in all this, and The Vizier is out there biding his time."

"He will make himself known when the time is right for him. Until then, we must keep you safe."

I leaned forward and kissed him, knowing that our

kisses were limited. It wasn't just me in danger; it was Genie too, and if I didn't figure out how to stop it, the entire kingdom. A knock on the door broke us apart.

"Who is it?"

The voice of one of the guards came through the door. "Your Highness, I was asked to come and find you. Mr. Jamal and Ms. Freya are holding a meeting with the palace advisors. They thought you might like to attend."

I looked toward Genie, who nodded.

"I'll read through these books and see if I can find a recipe for memory elixirs. You go and rule the kingdom."

I followed the guard to the meeting room where Jamal and Freya sat, not quite at the head of the table. My parents' chairs sat empty.

Despite their seating positions, it was clear that Jamal and Freya were leading the meeting. There was something about them, the calm confidence that made them natural leaders. They were doing a better job than I was, and it showed.

"Gaia!" Jamal said, standing up and walking around the table. He kissed me quickly on the cheek. "Your mother isn't well. I've had the court physician look at her, but it seems it's just tiredness. She's resting. I thought we should try and get a grip on what's happening in the kingdom and try to put it back in some order. I know you and Freya have had some thoughts on the other kingdoms, but if we don't keep on top of everything here, then none of that will matter. I'm afraid all the seats are taken, but I'm sure your parents won't mind you using their seats."

Something had changed between us. The awkwardness and resentment had gone. It probably had more to do with his and Freya's burgeoning relationship rather than anything I had done, but it was nice. I sat in my mother's chair, leaving my father's empty.

Freya gave me a nod and a smile and stood to address the advisors. There were ten of them altogether. Six women and four men. All of them had been working in the palace for years. Without fear, Freya spoke.

"Ladies and gentlemen, as you know, Badalah is in crisis. The town of Kisbu is at the center of that crisis. The Sultan and Sultana are unable to rule at the moment, so we are going to have to work together and keep the kingdom going until we can solve the whys and wherefores of what is happening."

"There isn't a Sultan," one of the advisors pointed out.

"Who are you to tell us what we should be doing?" another one said. "You are a maid. We aren't here to draw baths and make beds."

I saw Jamal's lip twitch. He made to stand, but I placed my hand on his arm to stop him. Instead, I stood up.

"Freya and Jamal are here because of me. As the Sultana's daughter, you have to listen to me. I've picked Jamal and Freya to help me run this kingdom, and I want you to show them the respect they deserve. Freya was my maid. It's true, but unless you are blind, you'll notice that she has been instrumental in stopping the disaster that befell us when my mother decided to raise taxes. I didn't see any of you helping with the feasts for the people. Freya was at both.

Without Freya and Jamal, this kingdom would have fallen weeks ago."

I waited to see the advisors' reactions, but they remained silent. What could they say? Jamal and Freya had done a lot more than any of them had over the past weeks. Not that I could blame them. I recognized the dazed look in their eyes. They probably didn't know who they were, let alone what their jobs were.

Jamal spoke. "We are in the middle of something unlike anything we have seen before. I might have no royal blood running through my veins, but I have something that the majority of the people of Badalah do not. I have immunity to the magic that is polluting the atmosphere. How many of you have experienced disorientation these past weeks? How many of you have forgotten things you shouldn't? How many of you have found yourself talking to people who know you, but you have forgotten them?"

Around the table, the advisors began to raise their hands. First one or two, then all of them.

"This is a magical force that is sweeping through Badalah. It is the source of all our problems. Three weeks ago, Badalah was a flourishing kingdom with few problems. You might not remember, but there was a Sultan as well as the Sultana. My aim isn't to get us back to the state Badalah once was. I believe only Sultan Aladdin and Sultana Jawahir can do that. I am but a farmer and businessman, but I do plan to do my best to keep Badalah going through this mess until a time when both Aladdin and Jawahir recover from this magical madness. I need to know you will help with that to the best of your abilities. We are all on the same side. The fight is ours, not against ourselves, but against the person who brought this magic among us. The former Sultan's Vizier. The same one who tried to bring down the kingdom all those years ago."

Around the table, I heard the sharp intake of breath. Not all of them remembered The Vizier, but it was clear some of them did.

I had half a mind to get up and applaud Jamal's speech, but he was talking again. I listened as he spoke, marveling at how he held his audience captive by his words. His plan was simple. Start a publicity campaign to recruit people of magic to help us run the Kingdom.

I listened in awe as he set out a timeline of when he wanted everything done by. The advisors listened, and even more, they wrote down everything he said.

When the meeting was over, I waited until the advisors had left the room before speaking to him.

"You were magnificent!" I said. Next to him, Freya beamed with pride.

"It was Freya's idea," he said, glancing her way. I caught his smile as he looked at her.

"People around here have been fearful of magic for too long," she said. "But we can only fight magic if we have it. I don't know if anyone in Badalah has magic in the way you do, but there must be people like Jamal and I that are immune to what is going on. We need to build an army of people who remember the city, remember the kingdom, and remember how things used to be."

"We just need to convince people to come forward. Magic has been a taboo subject in Badalah for as long as I can remember. We might not get as many people as we would like." Jamal added.

"What are you going to do with all these people when you recruit them?"

Jamal took a deep breath and looked at Freya, who nodded her encouragement.

"We thought we'd send them out to the other towns and cities of Badalah and recruit more. The more people we have that remember the way things used to be, the more chance we have of getting it back that way."

I lowered my head, guilt weighing heavily on my shoulders. "I'm sorry. I should be doing more. I should have done more."

"No!" Freya said. "We purposely didn't come to you with this because you were doing the one thing only you could. We know this magic is something to do with you, and we think that only you can stop it. We can keep things going, but you are the only person that can end this. You need to figure out how to solve this while we do what we can here."

"But I don't know how. I know it's something to do with me, and it's something to do with The Vizier, but I don't know what. I think it's actually bigger than that too."

"Bigger than The Vizier?" Freya's eyes widened as though she could think of nothing worse than The Vizier.

I walked around the table, pushing in chairs. "A woman killed the midwife who was at my birth, not The Vizier. It's too much of a coincidence that she was murdered as this all started."

Jamal clicked his teeth. "But you don't know who the woman is. It could be anyone."

"I know," I admitted. "I need Genie's help to figure it all out, but his memory comes and goes like everyone else's. I need someone with his mind to help me figure out what's going on."

Jamal didn't even flinch when I mentioned Genie's name. I took it to be a good sign.

"I don't know how to help you get his mind back. If we could do that, we wouldn't be in this problem in the first place."

"Actually, I think there might be a way. I've been reading up on The Forge. They make potions there. There might be a potion for memory loss."

"Even magical memory loss?" Jamal asked.

I shrugged. "I don't know, but there is only one way to find out. I'm going to The Forge."

7TH JULY

A hard rapping on my door woke me from my slumber. Asher squawked as the knocking intensified, hammering persistently.

"What is it?" I replied, wiping the sleep from my eyes with the back of my fist as I pulled myself out of bed. I opened the door to find Jamal standing there, his eyes full of panic.

"Get dressed," he ordered, "We need you."

"What's the matter?" I asked, fear already churning in my stomach. Sparks began to fly from my skin, taking us both by surprise. I ignited my hand and let the magical fire burn to rid myself of the buildup of magical energy brought on by the sudden panic.

Jamal's eyes traveled to my hand, and I had to snap the fingers of my other hand to get his attention back. "Jamal. What is happening?"

Before he had a chance to answer, a group of guards ran past us. I watched as they raced down the corridor and out of view.

"People are being recruited," he said, almost absent-mindedly.

"I know. That was the plan, right?"

"Not by us," Jamal said, taking my hand in his as the other one flamed. "By The Vizier."

I felt weak, and the flame went out. "The Vizier? What do you mean he's recruiting people? He wants people of magic too?"

Jamal shook his head. "Get dressed and meet me in the entrance hall. I need to get the guards out. I'll see you in ten minutes."

With that, he took off down the hallway after the guards. I rushed to my wardrobe and threw on some pants and a shirt before running down to the entrance hall.

Freya stood by the open door as Jamal issued orders, sending the guards out to different parts of town.

"Anyone want to explain to me what is going on?" I asked as the last of the guards sprinted out of the door.

"He's after the lamp," Freya said, shutting the main doors. "The Vizier. He's looking for the lamp. He wants Genie."

My heart leapt into my throat at the thought of it. He'd tried and failed to get the lamp before. Getting it now would be disastrous. I was Genie's master because I was the first person to see him when he turned back into his magical self. I'd lose that right if someone rubbed the lamp.

I turned, ready to race to Genie, but Jamal grabbed my arm.

"You can't help him by being with him. We need to

come up with a way to stop The Vizier from getting the lamp. I've got almost all the guards out looking for him, but so far there have been no sightings."

"Then how do you know?"

"We got word this morning that someone had been approached in a bar in one of the seedier parts of town. He was asked to go into the desert and into a secret cave to get a lamp."

"My father found the lamp in a secret cave. He didn't throw it back there."

"Gaia. The lamp is magic. Just because your father didn't go back to the cave himself, doesn't mean the lamp didn't return there. Without Genie living in it, it is free to return."

"You speak as though it's a sentient being. It's a lamp."

Freya walked over and placed her hand on my arm. "It's a magic lamp. You might have magic, but you don't know much about it. I've read the history of the lamp. It was a myth even eighteen years ago. No one really believed it was anything other than a story, but The Vizier did. That's why he spent his life searching for it. Your father freeing Genie would have stopped The Vizier from using Genie's magic to become all-powerful if you hadn't have stopped him first. I believe that the lamp is back in the cave where your father found it. Just like back then, The Vizier is recruiting people to go and find it."

"I need to free Genie!" I said, breaking away from both of them. "It's the only way."

I ran from them, my head spinning. I couldn't let

The Vizier become Genie's master. There was no telling what havoc it would wreak, and if I lost my chance to free Genie, he would never get that chance again.

I ran into his room to find him drinking coffee at his desk. He stood when I barged in.

"Gaia, Whatever is the matter?" He pulled me into his arms as I began to shake.

"I need to free you. The Vizier is recruiting people to find the lamp."

Genie sucked in a breath and held me at arm's length. "The Vizier is here? In Kisbu? You're sure?"

"I think so," I answered, tears streaming down my face. "No one has seen him exactly, but someone saw a man trying to get people to go into the desert to find the lamp. It must be The Vizier. Who else could it be?"

The genie licked his lips and drummed his fingers on my arms, making his chains rattle.

"If The Vizier really is in town, then freeing me is the last thing you should do. I have powers now. They are limited without wishes, but I have them. Let me keep you safe, then if you do need to make that last wish, you can use it."

"No!" I cried out, frustration bubbling in my veins. "If he finds that lamp, it will be dangerous for us all. I won't have the last wish anymore. He'll have all the wishes, and he will use them against us."

Genie began to pace up and down the room. "He won't find it!"

"How could you possibly know that?" I cried out. "He found it before. He knows it's in the secret cave, and he knows where that cave is. Don't underestimate him. It is because of him you have these chains binding your wrists together. He is powerful enough to make you turn back into a genie."

Genie shook his head sadly. "And so if you use your last wish and make me a human, what is to stop him turning me into a genie again?"

I opened my mouth to answer, but the truth was horrifying. The Vizier was already powerful enough to make Genie a genie again. It didn't matter how many times I wished for him to be free. As long as The Vizier was alive, Genie would always be a slave.

"Then, we have to find the lamp before The Vizier does!"

"You don't even know where the cave is, Gaia. Even if you did, do you really think you'd be able to get the lamp out? Your father was incredibly lucky to survive. I can't put you in that danger."

I screamed in frustration. There was nothing I could do, and it was killing me. Genie held his hands up to my face and wiped the tears away with his thumbs. The chains hung down between us. I'd never felt more resentful of them as I did now. He lifted them and put his arms over my head then pulled me into a kiss. His lips were wet and tasted of salt, my own tears. With each new tear that fell, he kissed it away.

"We really can't stop this, huh?" I whispered.

"We can stop it, and we will. I just don't know how. We defeated The Vizier before, we'll do it again."

"I defeated him before," I reminded him, "but I don't know how. How can the birth of someone destroy someone else?"

Genie pulled the chains back over my head and went back to his desk where there was a huge stack of books, most of which were open.

"I don't know," he said, running his hands through his hair. "It takes a lot to stump me, but there are so many unknowns. The Vizier is more powerful now than he was before. I don't think he'd be able to turn me back into a Genie with only his own power. He must have someone helping him."

"A woman!" I said, perching on the edge of the desk. "The woman that killed the midwife. But we don't know who she is."

"No, we don't. Then there is the puzzle of how you defeated The Vizier. You and your siblings. We don't even know how many you have."

We had so many puzzle pieces that didn't fit together. "Can't you remember where the cave was? You lived there. Surely you could take us to the cave, and we could retrieve the lamp ourselves?"

Genie closed his eyes and placed his head in his hands. "I barely remember what I had for breakfast anymore. You are asking me to remember things, but my memory is gone. I don't know." He slammed his fist down on the table and shouted. "I don't know."

"I can't do this," I said, turning around and leaving his room. When I was outside, I leaned against his door and burst into tears.

Everything was hopeless. If Genie couldn't save us all, who could? Jamal and Freya were trying, but the odds against them were insurmountable. Even if they did find some people with latent magic and they were able to convince them to come to the palace, then what?

Genie was once the most powerful person in the whole kingdom. I probably was the most powerful person in the kingdom now, but none of that helped me in my current situation. If The Vizier got the lamp, we were all doomed.

I wiped my eyes on the back of my hands and tried to pull myself together. If only Genie remembered everything, I was sure that he'd be able to figure all this out. He was a genius. He was just lost like the rest of us.

If he wasn't going to let me wish him free, I was going to free him another way. I strode down the corridor to my own room and quickly packed a bag of clothes.

"Where are you going?" Freya asked after walking into my room and catching me in the act.

I ignored her question. "I know you are not my maid anymore, but would you please run to the kitchen and ask them to pack me some food. I've not eaten today, and I'm starving."

She stood, her feet wide and her arms crossed. "Not unless you tell me where you are going. You are going to the desert, aren't you? You think you can find the lamp."

I pulled my bag over my shoulder and approached her. "Freya. I'm not going anywhere unsafe. I'm not going to the desert."

"So where then?"

"I told you already. I'm going to The Forge."

Her eyes opened wide in surprise. "I didn't expect you to go so soon. And for a potion? Surely they can't make enough for a whole kingdom?"

If it wasn't so serious, I would have laughed. "No.

For Genie. He will figure all this out. You know how intelligent he is. He just needs to remember."

She nodded. "That's not a bad idea. I can't let you go alone, though. It's not safe."

"Genie's coming with me," I lied. I'd never lied to her before, but she and Jamal were busy enough without having to babysit me. Hopefully, by the time Freya realized that Genie was bound to the palace, I'd already be gone.

As Freya went to the kitchens, I went to say goodbye to my mother. She was sitting up in bed, staring at the wall opposite her. She didn't even acknowledge my presence as I kissed her cheek.

"I'm going to find a memory potion!" I whispered to her. "I'll bring some back for you and for father too."

She murmured an incoherent reply, almost breaking my heart in the process.

Freya caught up with me by the staff entrance. "When will you be home?" she asked tears in her eyes. I pulled her into a hug. "I'm not going to be gone long. I'll find the elixir and come straight home."

She nodded as she handed over the food. "I got enough for you and Genie."

"He's just outside," I lied. "I trust you and Jamal to keep the kingdom running. You two are doing a better job than I ever could."

She snorted a laugh between the tears. "I don't know about that. We are just doing our duty."

"When this is all over, I'll make sure the pair of you are recognized for your efforts."

"We need this to all be over first," Freya reminded me.

I gave her one last hug and slipped out of the door.

I hated that I was running away. Neither Genie nor Jamal knew that I was going. My plan was to get the first airship out, find the elixir, and come straight back. If things went to plan, I'd be two days, max.

I kept to the shadows as I ran through the back-streets to the Urbis Express station. I'd already checked the timetable. There was one due to leave for The Forge within the hour. I'd brought enough money with me to use the royal cabin if I had to, but I hoped there was enough space for me to travel in the main cabin.

I barely noticed the shadow that crossed my path, but the sudden thickness of the air squeezed my lungs. My whole body began to tingle with magical energy. I'd felt it once before in Kisbu, and it had turned out to be nothing.

I stood, darting my head around, quickly searching for the source of the magic. I already knew who it was. I could feel him, feel the malevolent force his magic generated, but it was only when he stepped out of the shadows that I stopped. The whole world suddenly seemed darker as though the sun had gone behind a cloud, and the ambient noises of the busy Kisbu streets had silenced. A chill invaded the air.

"What do you want?" I shouted out to The Vizier as he walked slowly to the middle of the alley about fifty feet from where I was standing.

"You know what I want, Gaia."

His voice was low, and yet, I could hear him even with the space between us. Even that was carried by magic. I looked around, hoping that someone would walk into the street, but it was unusually quiet, even for Kisbu's back streets.

"You want me. Why?"

"I believe I told you why when we were fortunate to cross paths in Urbis," he said, taking a slow step forward. With each step, he moved closer. I stumbled a step backward.

"You told me that my siblings and I defeated you. How do you know so much about me?"

"I know everything there is to know about you, Princess Gaia, you and your mother. It's an interesting story. It's a shame that you'll never get to know it."

He pulled his arm back and sent a jet of purple light in my direction. Instinct had me ducking just in time. I fell to the ground and rolled into a narrow alley. The second I was out of his view, I jumped to my feet and ran. I'd fought him before. I had no intention of doing it again. The alley took me into a residential district away from the airship station I'd been heading toward. Clothes hanging on lines crisscrossed the street forcing me to duck every few feet, slowing me down. I could no longer see The Vizier behind me, but his magic remained as strong as ever. At the end of the alley, I skirted a building and turned into a street I hoped would take me to one of Kisbu's main streets in the hope that he wouldn't follow me if there were witnesses.

After fifteen minutes of running, I stopped and allowed myself a rest. Taking a few deep breaths, I looked back. The Vizier was nowhere to be seen, but I knew he was behind me somewhere. The street I was on looked vaguely familiar. It was one of the ones I sometimes took on my nighttime rambles.

The spice market was close by. If I could get there, he'd never find me in the throng of shoppers. Not waiting for him to appear, I took off again, running this time on more familiar ground. Except when I got to the spice market, there was no one there. The spices and wares were covered over, closed for the day. Looking up, I saw that the evening had come quickly. Way too quickly. I'd left the palace in the afternoon. By my calculations, I'd been out just over half an hour. There was no way it could be evening, and yet the darkening of the sky told me it was. Had The Vizier altered time itself or had he messed with my mind in the way he'd messed with anyone else's. The thought of it scared me more than anything else. I was saved thinking about it too much by the bright colors of spices filling the air in an explosion of powder.

I took off again, winding through the alleys of the stalls, tears streaming down my face from the sting of the spices in my eyes and my lungs straining to breathe.

I ran, almost blindly through the market, feeling my way as the noise of stalls being hit by magic got closer and closer.

Each breath I inhaled burned at my lungs, but I didn't slow down. To slow down would be my inevitable demise, and yet, the pain of going forward almost had me falling to my knees.

Fighting fire with fire, literally, in this case, I shot out flames blindly behind me.

Everything, beyond the sound of the spice market

going up in magic, was silent. Where were the people? This area of Kisbu was a hub, and even in the early evening would be full of people heading home from their work. Something was wrong, but without being able to see, I didn't know what.

I tripped over something, and fell forward. Holding my arms out in front of me to soften the fall, I was surprised to find myself plunging into water. Panic enveloped me as I tried to make sense of it. For a brief second, I thought I'd fallen into a river before sense prevailed, and I remembered that no rivers ran through Kisbu. As my face hit the water, the spices cleared from my eyes, and I was able to see. Sitting up in the knee-deep water, I found that I could see again. I'd fallen in a water trough meant for drinking water for horses and camels. I was soaking, but I was alive. The sun had fallen further in the sky. In front of the burning orb, the familiar silhouette of The Vizier appeared. I couldn't get out of the water quick enough. Water slopped out of the sides of the trough as I tried to move. The sun was entirely blocked out as The Vizier stepped closer.

I waited for the inevitable, but it never came. Instead, something happened that chilled me much more than my own death.

"You know, I think killing you right away would be a mistake," The Vizier mused. "Your father found me the lamp all those years ago. How fitting it would be to use you to get it for me now."

He leaned forward and grabbed the front of my shirt, pulling me from the water.

His menacing eyes glared at me as he held me up to his eye level, levitating me from the ground.

"You, my dear, are going to get Genie for me. You are going to help me bring about the downfall of Badalah." And with that, he heaved me over his shoulder and began to carry me to the edge of town.

Read more in Goddess of Fire

SPECIAL OFFER

We hope you enjoyed reading this book.

To thank you for reading, we'd like to offer you a discount on our other Kingdom of Fairytale books

Go to www.jaarmitage.com and add the code KOF10 for 10% your full order.

The discount is a one time offer, but will include as many books as you add to your first order.

A NOTE FROM THE AUTHOR

The Kingdom of Fairytales authors hope you enjoyed this new way of reading. We don't think that a series has ever been set with one chapter a day thought a whole year before and we hope we did it justice.

With this in mind, please leave a review, but when you do, remember that these books were always meant to be short breaks in your day and the blurb reflects that.

ABOUT J.A. ARMITAGE

J.A. Armitage lives in a total fantasy world (because reality is boring right?) When she's not writing all the crazy fun in her head, she can be found eating cake, designing pretty pictures and hanging upside down from the tallest climbing frame in the local playground while her children look on in embarrassment. She's travelled the world working as everything from a banana picker in Australia to a Pantomime clown, has climbed to the top of Mount Kilimanjaro and the bottom of the Grand Canyon and once gave birth to a surrogate baby for a friend of hers.

She spends way too much time gossiping on face-book and if you want to be part of her Reading Army, where you'll get lots of freebies, exclusive sneak peeks and super secret sales, find her on Kingdom of Fairy-tales on Facebook

https://www.facebook.com/KingdomofFairytales

And for more books, check out:

www.jaarmitage.com

ALSO BY J.A. ARMITAGE

REVERSE FAIRYTALES CINDERELLA

Charm: A Cinderella Reverse Fairytale book 1

Lucky Charm: A Cinderella Reverse Fairytale book 2

Charmed

Charm: Books 1-3 boxset

REVERSE FAIRYTALES LITTLE MERMAID

Dark Water: A Little Mermaid Reverse Fairytale

Blue Water

Breakwater

Dark Water: Books 1-3 the full series

DRAGON TAMER

Slayer

Warrior

Protector

Savior

Dragon Tamer Boxset

Dragon Tamer colouring book

THE FAERIE RACE

The Sorcery Trial: A Fae Adventure Romance

The Elemental Trial: A Fae Adventure Romance

The Doomsday Trial: A Fae Adventure Romance

The Faerie Race: The Complete Fae Adventure Romance Series

REALM OF FIRE AND LIGHT

The Unicorn Key: A Dark Fae Adventure

The Unicorn Quest: A Dark Fae Adventure

The Unicorn Secret: A Dark Fae Adventure

KINGDOM OF FAIRYTALES

Queen of Dragons: A Sleeping Beauty retelling

Heiress of Embers: A Sleeping Beauty retelling

Throne of Fury: A Sleeping Beauty retelling

Goddess of Flames: A Sleeping Beauty retelling

Queen of mermaids: A Little Mermaid retelling

Heiress of the Sea: A Little Mermaid retelling

Throne of Change: A Little Mermaid retelling

Goddess of Water: A Little Mermaid retelling

King of Wolves: A Little Red Riding Hood retelling

Heir of the Curse: A Little Red Riding Hood retelling

Throne of Night: A Little Red Riding Hood retelling

God of Shifters: A Little Red Riding Hood retelling

King of Devotion: A Rapunzel retelling

Heir of Thorns: A Rapunzel retelling

Throne of Enchantment: A Rapunzel retelling

God of Loyalty: A Rapunzel retelling

Queen of Unicorns: A Rumpelstiltskin retelling

Heiress of Gold: A Rumpelstiltskin retelling

Throne of Sacrifice: A Rumpelstiltskin retelling

Goddess of Loss: A Rumpelstiltskin retelling

King of Beasts: A Beauty and the Beast retelling

Heir of Beauty: A Beauty and the Beast retelling

Throne of Betrayal: A Beauty and the Beast retelling

God of Illusion: A Beauty and the Beast retelling

Queen of the Sun: An Aladdin retelling

Heiress of Shadows: An Aladdin retelling

Throne of the Phoenix: An Aladdin Retelling

Goddess of Fire: An Aladdin retelling

Queen of Song: A Cinderella Retelling

Heiress of Melody: A Cinderella retelling

Throne of Symphony: A Cinderella retelling

Goddess of Harmony: A Cinderella Retelling

Queen of Clockwork: An Alice in Wonderland retelling

Heiress of Delusion: An Alice in Wonderland retelling

Throne of Cards: An Alice in Wonderland retelling

Goddess of Hearts: An Alice in Wonderland retelling

King of Traitors: A Wizard of Oz retelling

Heir of Fugitives: A Wizard of Oz retelling

Throne of Emeralds: A Wizard of Oz retelling

God of Storms: A Wizard of Oz retelling

Queen of Reflections: A Snow White retelling

Heiress of Mirrors: A Snow White retelling

Throne of Wands: A Snow White retelling

Goddess of Magic: A Snow White retelling

Queen of Skies: A Peter Pan retelling

Heiress of Stars: A Peter Pan retelling

Goddess of Air: A Peter Pan retelling

Throne of Feathers: A Peter Pan retelling

Kingdom of Power

Kingdom of Royalty

Kingdom of Fairytales

Kingdom of Ever After

Azia: Daughter of Sleeping Beauty

Blaise: Daughter of the Little Mermaid

Castiel: Son of Red Riding Hood

Deon: Son of Rapunzel

Eliana: Rapunzel's revenge

Fallon: Son of Beauty and the Beast

Gaia: Daughter of Aladdin

Halia: Daughter of Cinderella

Ivy: Daughter of Alice

Jakon:Son of Dorothy

Kelis: Daughter of Snow White

Lyric: Daughter of Peter Pan

Urbis: the final Fairytale

ABOUT R.CASTRO

A daughter, sister, wife, and most importantly, a mother.

R. Castro clings to her unwavering faith in God, as she treks through this journey called life.

Writing has encouraged her to step out of her comfort zone, as she continues enjoying the beautiful diversity our world has to offer.